D1091569

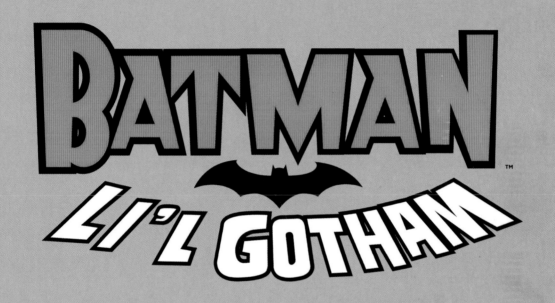

STONE ARCH BOOKS
a capstone imprint

STONE ARCH BOOKS™

Published in 2014 by Stone Arch Books
A Capstone Imprint
1710 Roe Crest Drive
North Mankato, MN 56003
www.capstonepub.com

Originally published by DC Comics in the U.S. in single
magazine form as Batman: Li'l Gotham.
Copyright © 2014 DC Comics. All Rights Reserved.

DC Comics
1700 Broadway, New York, NY 10019
A Warner Bros. Entertainment Company

Printed in China.
032014   008085LEOF14

Cataloging-in-Publication Data is available at the Library
of Congress website:
ISBN: 978-1-4342-9221-6 (library binding)

Summary: Pick up some flowers for mom this Mother's
Day, then head over to Li'l Gotham and join us as Damian
Wayne, Batman's son, searches for the true meaning of
family, the true value of friendship, and the maximum
amount of toppings Alfred can actually fit on a pizza!
Then, on Father's Day, Commissioner Gordon's favorite restaurant is overbooked, so they have to share a table with
some questionable company...a family of super-villains!

STONE ARCH BOOKS

Ashley C. Andersen Zantop **Publisher**
Michael Dahl **Editorial Director**
Sean Tulien **Editor**
Heather Kindseth **Creative Director**
Bob Lentz **Art Director**
Hilary Wacholz **Designer**
Kathy McColley **Production Specialist**

DC Comics

Joan Hilty & Harvey Richards **Original U.S. Editors**
Jeff Matsuda & Dave McCaig **Cover Artists**

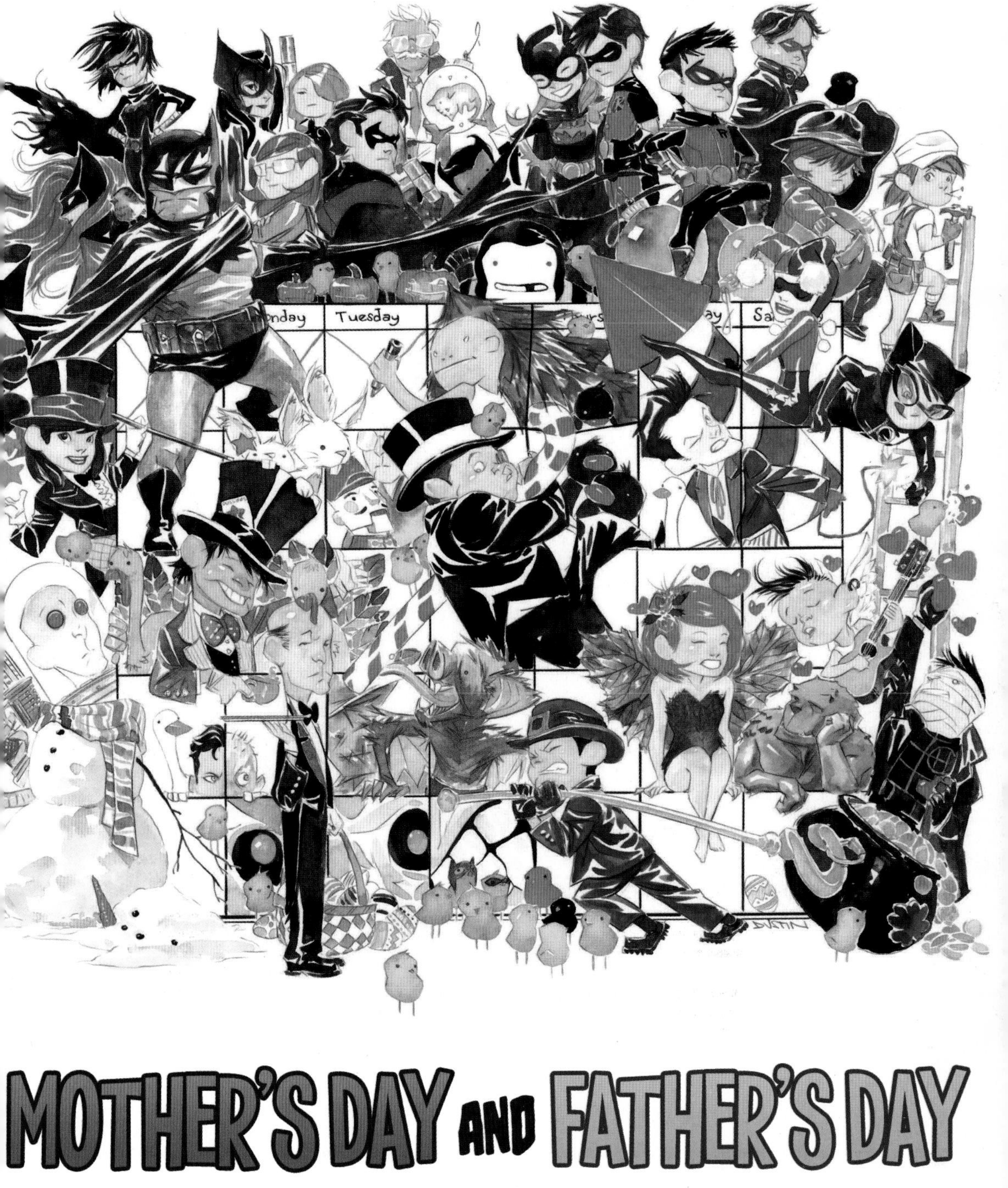
Tuesday

MOTHER'S DAY AND FATHER'S DAY

Dustin Nguyen & Derek Fridolfs...................... writers
Dustin Nguyen.. artist
Saida Temofonte.. letterer

BATMAN created by
Bob Kane

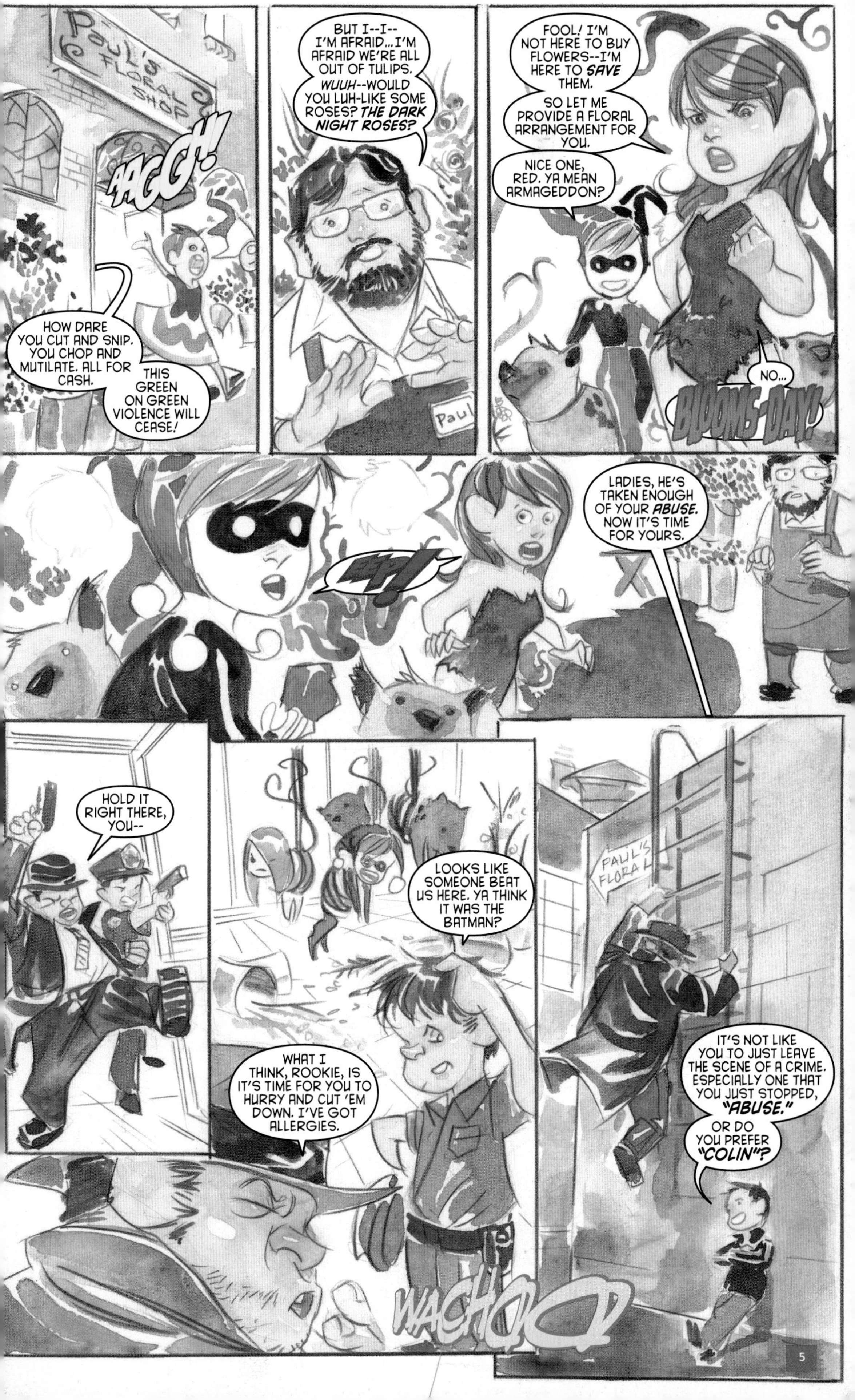
PAUL'S FLORAL SHOP
AAGGH!
HOW DARE YOU CUT AND SNIP. YOU CHOP AND MUTILATE. ALL FOR CASH.
THIS GREEN ON GREEN VIOLENCE WILL CEASE!
BUT I--I-- I'M AFRAID...I'M AFRAID WE'RE ALL OUT OF TULIPS. WUUH--WOULD YOU LUH-LIKE SOME ROSES? THE DARK NIGHT ROSES?
PAUL
FOOL! I'M NOT HERE TO BUY FLOWERS--I'M HERE TO SAVE THEM.
SO LET ME PROVIDE A FLORAL ARRANGEMENT FOR YOU.
NICE ONE, RED. YA MEAN ARMAGEDDON?
NO...
BLOOMS-DAY!
EEP!
LADIES, HE'S TAKEN ENOUGH OF YOUR ABUSE. NOW IT'S TIME FOR YOURS.
HOLD IT RIGHT THERE, YOU--
LOOKS LIKE SOMEONE BEAT US HERE. YA THINK IT WAS THE BATMAN?
WHAT I THINK, ROOKIE, IS IT'S TIME FOR YOU TO HURRY AND CUT 'EM DOWN. I'VE GOT ALLERGIES.
WACHOO!
PAUL'S FLORAL
IT'S NOT LIKE YOU TO JUST LEAVE THE SCENE OF A CRIME. ESPECIALLY ONE THAT YOU JUST STOPPED, "ABUSE."
OR DO YOU PREFER "COLIN"?

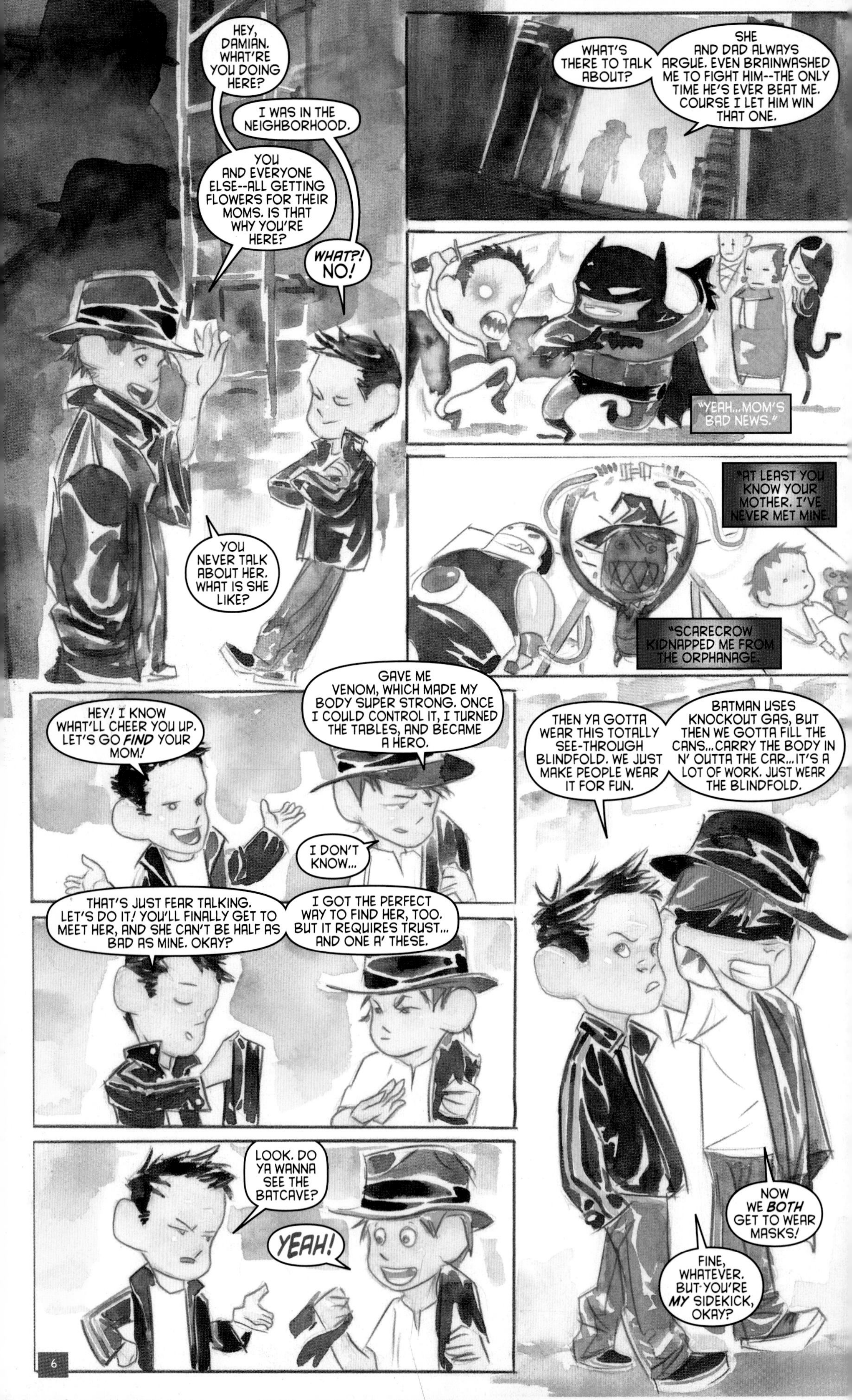
HEY, DAMIAN. WHAT'RE YOU DOING HERE?
I WAS IN THE NEIGHBORHOOD.
YOU AND EVERYONE ELSE--ALL GETTING FLOWERS FOR THEIR MOMS. IS THAT WHY YOU'RE HERE?
WHAT?! NO!
YOU NEVER TALK ABOUT HER. WHAT IS SHE LIKE?
WHAT'S THERE TO TALK ABOUT?
SHE AND DAD ALWAYS ARGUE. EVEN BRAINWASHED ME TO FIGHT HIM--THE ONLY TIME HE'S EVER BEAT ME. COURSE I LET HIM WIN THAT ONE.
"YEAH...MOM'S BAD NEWS."
"AT LEAST YOU KNOW YOUR MOTHER. I'VE NEVER MET MINE.
"SCARECROW KIDNAPPED ME FROM THE ORPHANAGE.
GAVE ME VENOM, WHICH MADE MY BODY SUPER STRONG. ONCE I COULD CONTROL IT, I TURNED THE TABLES, AND BECAME A HERO.
HEY! I KNOW WHAT'LL CHEER YOU UP. LET'S GO FIND YOUR MOM!
I DON'T KNOW...
THAT'S JUST FEAR TALKING. LET'S DO IT! YOU'LL FINALLY GET TO MEET HER, AND SHE CAN'T BE HALF AS BAD AS MINE. OKAY?
I GOT THE PERFECT WAY TO FIND HER, TOO. BUT IT REQUIRES TRUST... AND ONE A' THESE.
LOOK. DO YA WANNA SEE THE BATCAVE?
YEAH!
BATMAN USES KNOCKOUT GAS, BUT THEN WE GOTTA FILL THE CANS...CARRY THE BODY IN N' OUTTA THE CAR...IT'S A LOT OF WORK. JUST WEAR THE BLINDFOLD.
THEN YA GOTTA WEAR THIS TOTALLY SEE-THROUGH BLINDFOLD. WE JUST MAKE PEOPLE WEAR IT FOR FUN.
NOW WE BOTH GET TO WEAR MASKS!
FINE, WHATEVER. BUT YOU'RE MY SIDEKICK, OKAY?

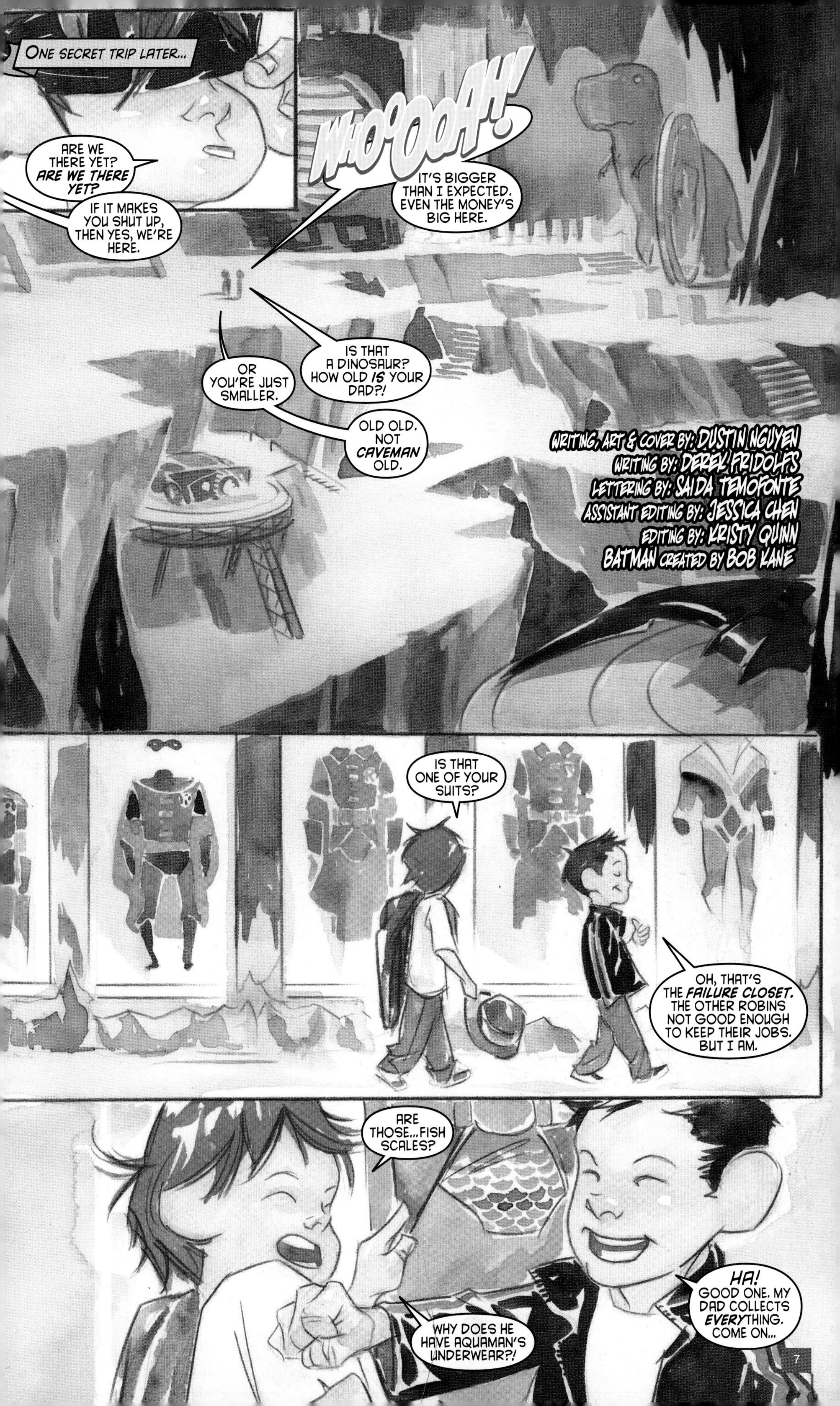
ONE SECRET TRIP LATER...
ARE WE THERE YET? ARE WE THERE YET?
IF IT MAKES YOU SHUT UP, THEN YES, WE'RE HERE.
WHOOOOAH!
IT'S BIGGER THAN I EXPECTED. EVEN THE MONEY'S BIG HERE.
IS THAT A DINOSAUR? HOW OLD IS YOUR DAD?!
OR YOU'RE JUST SMALLER.
OLD OLD. NOT CAVEMAN OLD.
WRITING, ART & COVER BY: DUSTIN NGUYEN
WRITING BY: DEREK FRIDOLFS
LETTERING BY: SAIDA TEMOFONTE
ASSISTANT EDITING BY: JESSICA CHEN
EDITING BY: KRISTY QUINN
BATMAN CREATED BY BOB KANE
IS THAT ONE OF YOUR SUITS?
OH, THAT'S THE FAILURE CLOSET. THE OTHER ROBINS NOT GOOD ENOUGH TO KEEP THEIR JOBS. BUT I AM.
ARE THOSE...FISH SCALES?
WHY DOES HE HAVE AQUAMAN'S UNDERWEAR?!
HA! GOOD ONE. MY DAD COLLECTS EVERYTHING. COME ON...

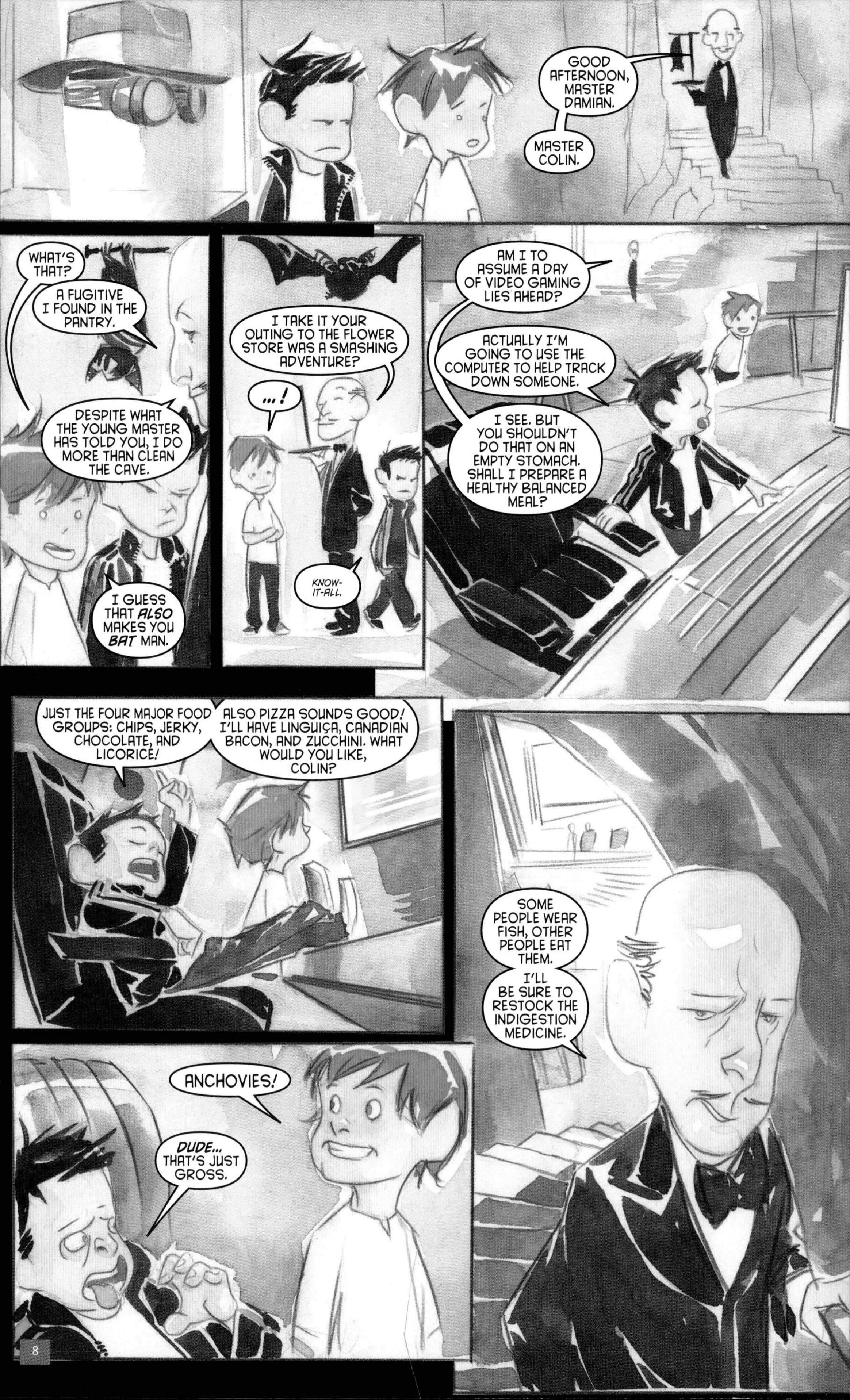
GOOD AFTERNOON, MASTER DAMIAN.
MASTER COLIN.
WHAT'S THAT?
A FUGITIVE I FOUND IN THE PANTRY.
DESPITE WHAT THE YOUNG MASTER HAS TOLD YOU, I DO MORE THAN CLEAN THE CAVE.
I GUESS THAT ALSO MAKES YOU BAT MAN.
I TAKE IT YOUR OUTING TO THE FLOWER STORE WAS A SMASHING ADVENTURE?
...!
KNOW-IT-ALL.
AM I TO ASSUME A DAY OF VIDEO GAMING LIES AHEAD?
ACTUALLY I'M GOING TO USE THE COMPUTER TO HELP TRACK DOWN SOMEONE.
I SEE. BUT YOU SHOULDN'T DO THAT ON AN EMPTY STOMACH. SHALL I PREPARE A HEALTHY BALANCED MEAL?
JUST THE FOUR MAJOR FOOD GROUPS: CHIPS, JERKY, CHOCOLATE, AND LICORICE!
ALSO PIZZA SOUNDS GOOD! I'LL HAVE LINGUIÇA, CANADIAN BACON, AND ZUCCHINI. WHAT WOULD YOU LIKE, COLIN?
ANCHOVIES!
DUDE... THAT'S JUST GROSS.
SOME PEOPLE WEAR FISH, OTHER PEOPLE EAT THEM.
I'LL BE SURE TO RESTOCK THE INDIGESTION MEDICINE.

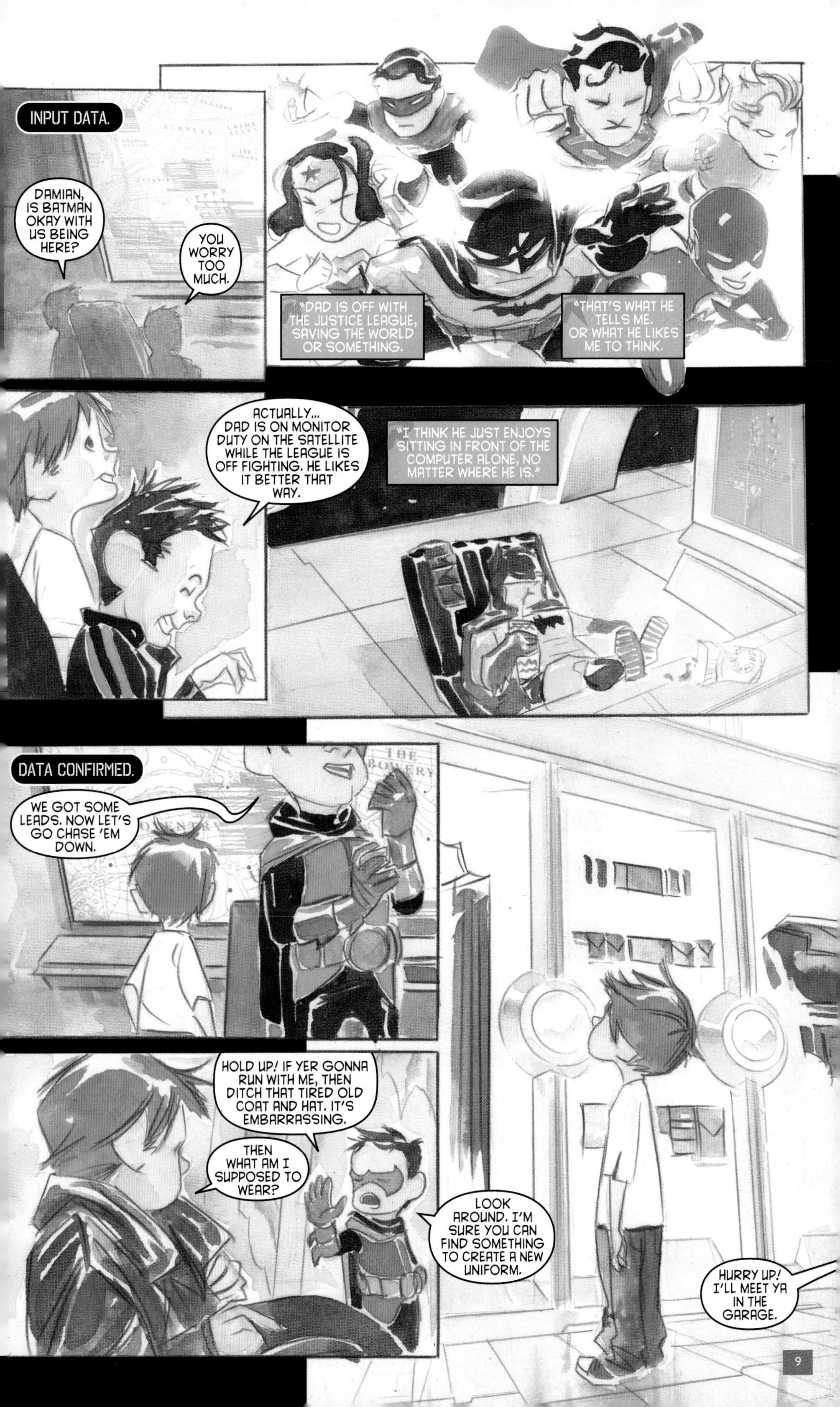

INPUT DATA.
DAMIAN, IS BATMAN OKAY WITH US BEING HERE?
YOU WORRY TOO MUCH.
"DAD IS OFF WITH THE JUSTICE LEAGUE, SAVING THE WORLD OR SOMETHING.
"THAT'S WHAT HE TELLS ME. OR WHAT HE LIKES ME TO THINK.
ACTUALLY... DAD IS ON MONITOR DUTY ON THE SATELLITE WHILE THE LEAGUE IS OFF FIGHTING. HE LIKES IT BETTER THAT WAY.
"I THINK HE JUST ENJOYS SITTING IN FRONT OF THE COMPUTER ALONE, NO MATTER WHERE HE IS."
DATA CONFIRMED.
WE GOT SOME LEADS. NOW LET'S GO CHASE 'EM DOWN.
HOLD UP! IF YER GONNA RUN WITH ME, THEN DITCH THAT TIRED OLD COAT AND HAT. IT'S EMBARRASSING.
THEN WHAT AM I SUPPOSED TO WEAR?
LOOK AROUND. I'M SURE YOU CAN FIND SOMETHING TO CREATE A NEW UNIFORM.
HURRY UP! I'LL MEET YA IN THE GARAGE.

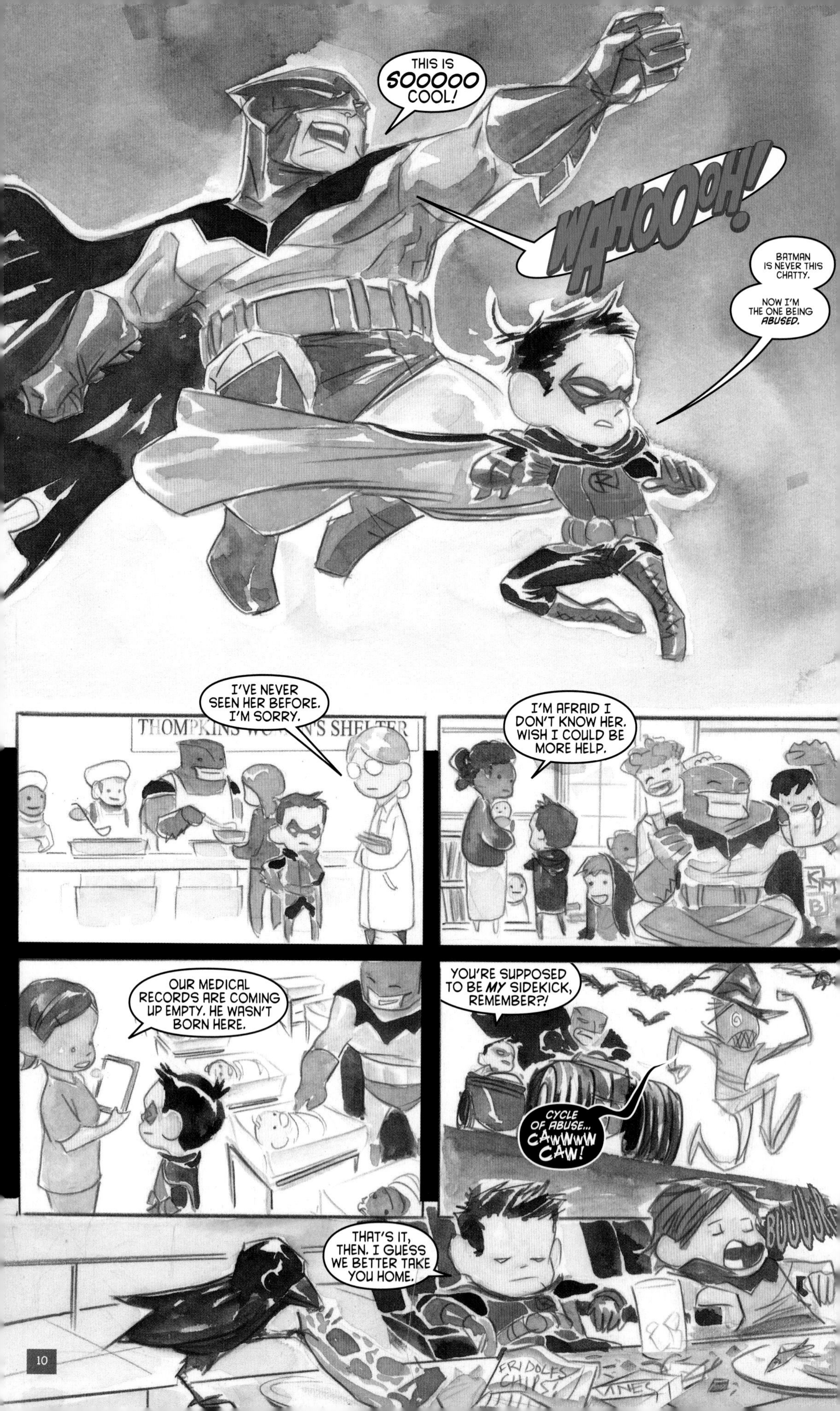

THIS IS SOOOOO COOL!
WAHOOOOH!
BATMAN IS NEVER THIS CHATTY.
NOW I'M THE ONE BEING ABUSED.
THOMPKINS WOMEN'S SHELTER
I'VE NEVER SEEN HER BEFORE. I'M SORRY.
I'M AFRAID I DON'T KNOW HER. WISH I COULD BE MORE HELP.
OUR MEDICAL RECORDS ARE COMING UP EMPTY. HE WASN'T BORN HERE.
YOU'RE SUPPOSED TO BE MY SIDEKICK, REMEMBER?!
CYCLE OF ABUSE... CAWWWW CAW!
THAT'S IT, THEN. I GUESS WE BETTER TAKE YOU HOME.

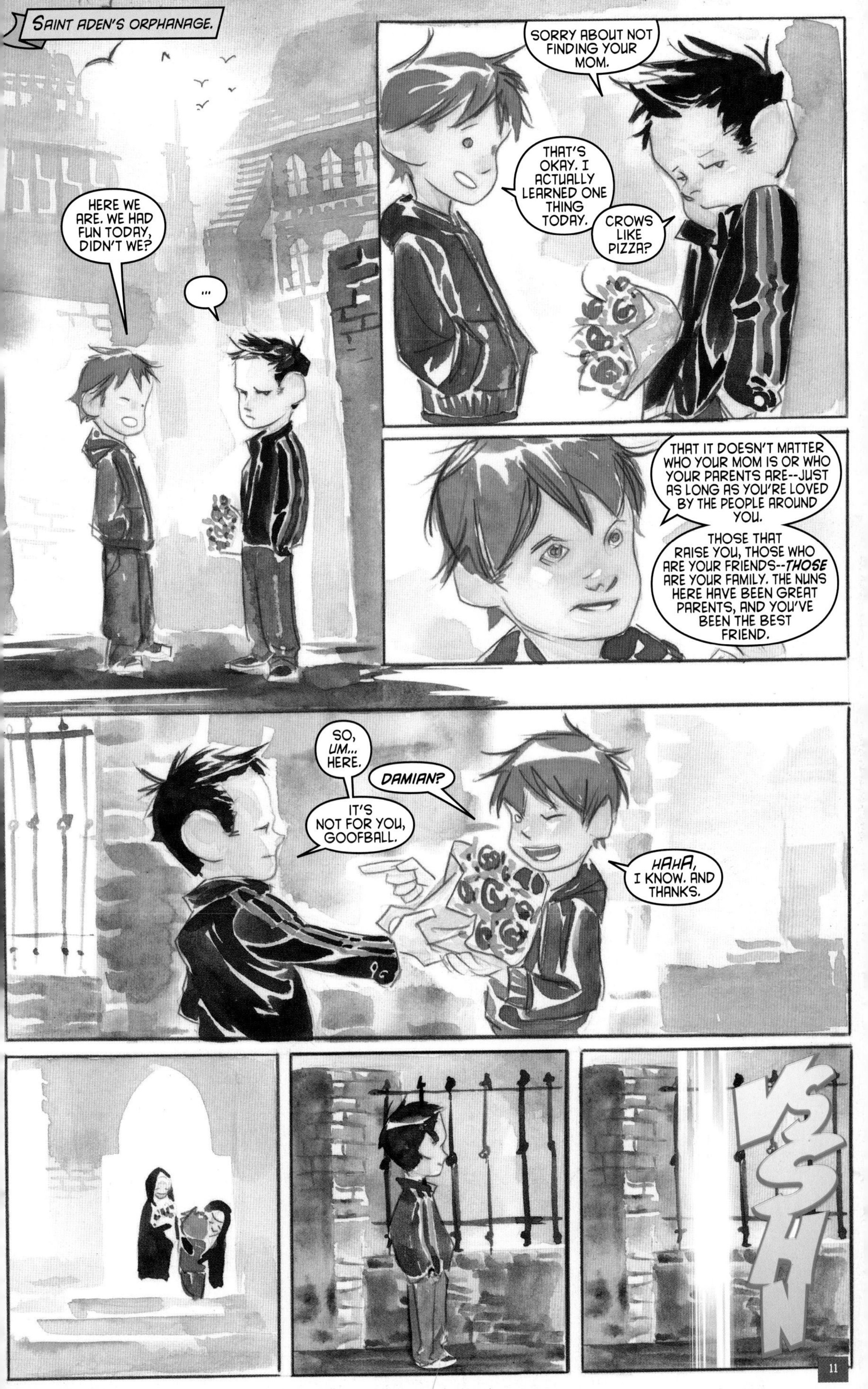
Saint Aden's orphanage.
HERE WE ARE. WE HAD FUN TODAY, DIDN'T WE?
...
SORRY ABOUT NOT FINDING YOUR MOM.
THAT'S OKAY. I ACTUALLY LEARNED ONE THING TODAY.
CROWS LIKE PIZZA?
THAT IT DOESN'T MATTER WHO YOUR MOM IS OR WHO YOUR PARENTS ARE--JUST AS LONG AS YOU'RE LOVED BY THE PEOPLE AROUND YOU.
THOSE THAT RAISE YOU, THOSE WHO ARE YOUR FRIENDS--THOSE ARE YOUR FAMILY. THE NUNS HERE HAVE BEEN GREAT PARENTS, AND YOU'VE BEEN THE BEST FRIEND.
SO, UM... HERE.
DAMIAN?
IT'S NOT FOR YOU, GOOFBALL.
HAHA, I KNOW. AND THANKS.
VSSHH

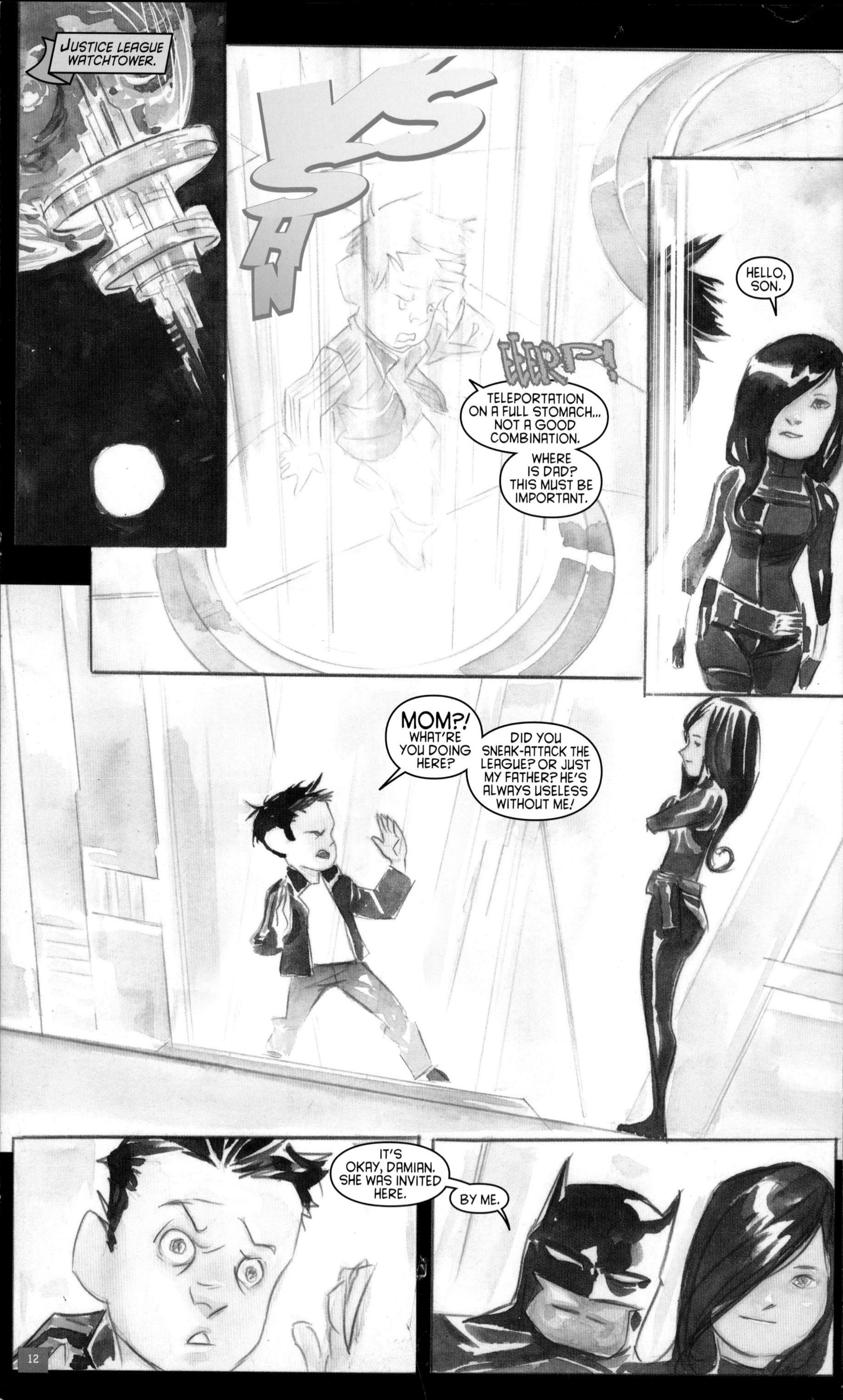
JUSTICE LEAGUE WATCHTOWER.
KSSHH
EEERP!
TELEPORTATION ON A FULL STOMACH... NOT A GOOD COMBINATION.
WHERE IS DAD? THIS MUST BE IMPORTANT.
HELLO, SON.
MOM?! WHAT'RE YOU DOING HERE?
DID YOU SNEAK-ATTACK THE LEAGUE? OR JUST MY FATHER? HE'S ALWAYS USELESS WITHOUT ME!
IT'S OKAY, DAMIAN. SHE WAS INVITED HERE.
BY ME.

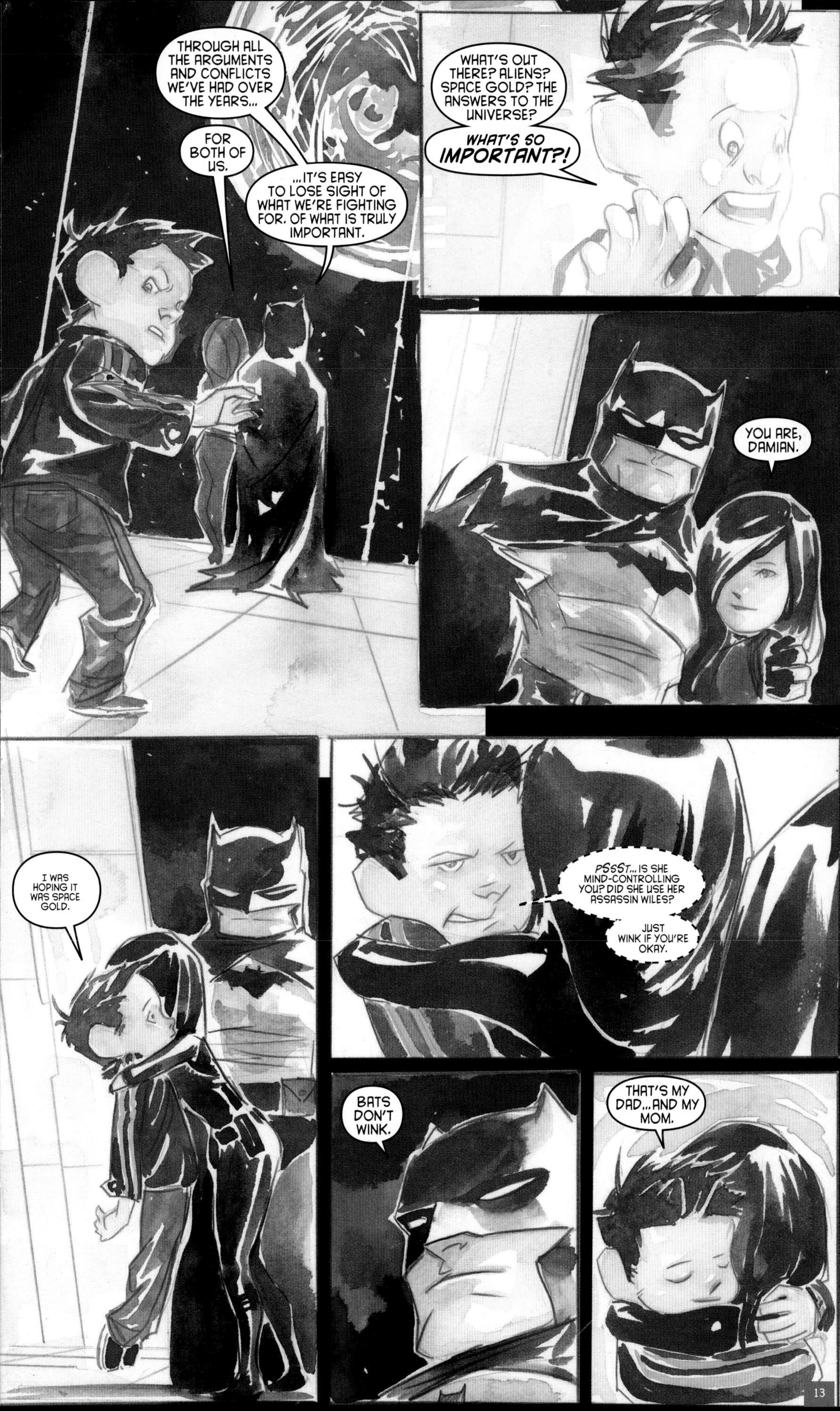
THROUGH ALL THE ARGUMENTS AND CONFLICTS WE'VE HAD OVER THE YEARS...
FOR BOTH OF US.
...IT'S EASY TO LOSE SIGHT OF WHAT WE'RE FIGHTING FOR. OF WHAT IS TRULY IMPORTANT.
WHAT'S OUT THERE? ALIENS? SPACE GOLD? THE ANSWERS TO THE UNIVERSE?
WHAT'S SO IMPORTANT?!
YOU ARE, DAMIAN.
I WAS HOPING IT WAS SPACE GOLD.
PSSST... IS SHE MIND-CONTROLLING YOU? DID SHE USE HER ASSASSIN WILES?
JUST WINK IF YOU'RE OKAY.
BATS DON'T WINK.
THAT'S MY DAD...AND MY MOM.

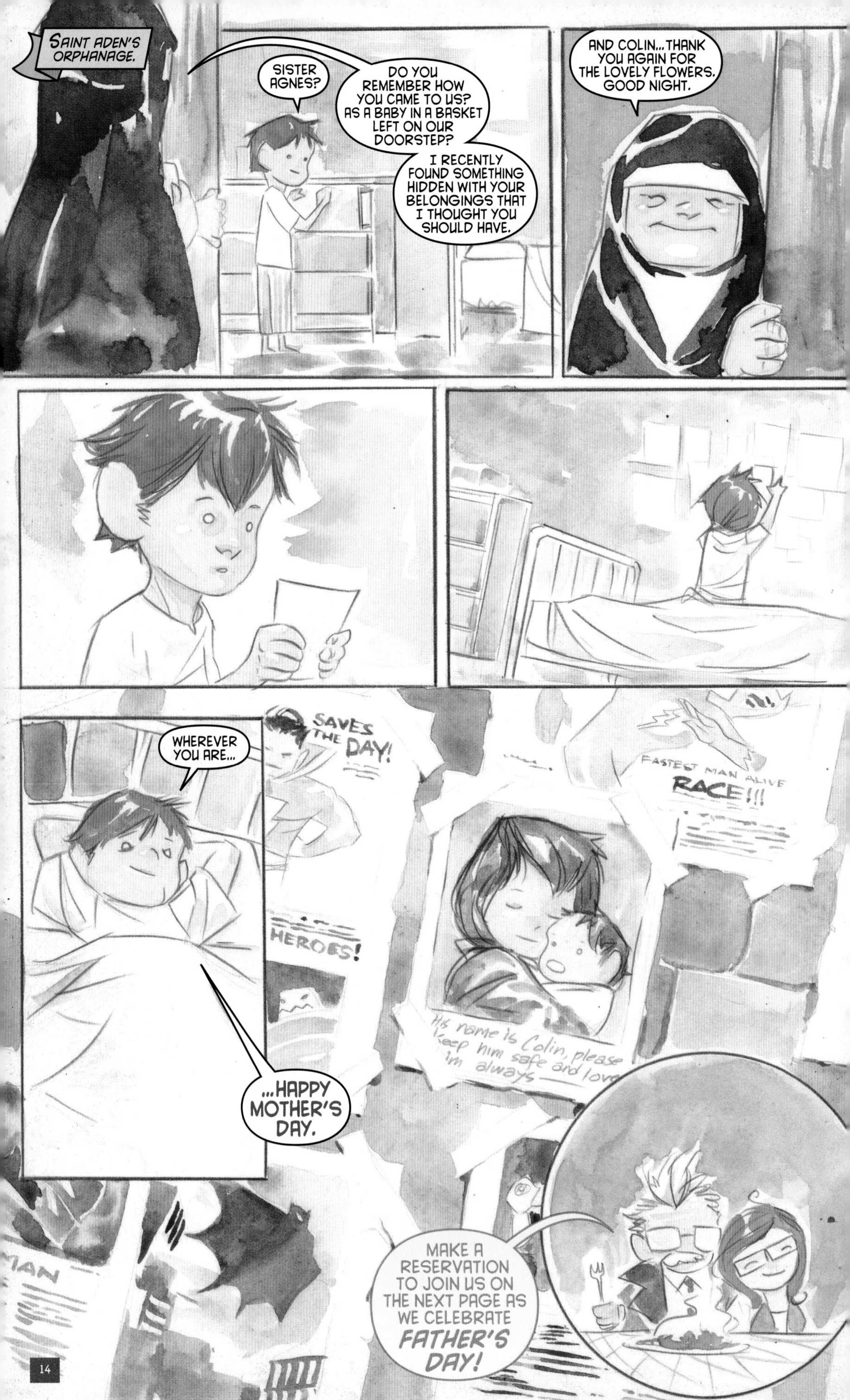
SAINT ADEN'S ORPHANAGE.
SISTER AGNES?
DO YOU REMEMBER HOW YOU CAME TO US? AS A BABY IN A BASKET LEFT ON OUR DOORSTEP?
I RECENTLY FOUND SOMETHING HIDDEN WITH YOUR BELONGINGS THAT I THOUGHT YOU SHOULD HAVE.
AND COLIN... THANK YOU AGAIN FOR THE LOVELY FLOWERS. GOOD NIGHT.
WHEREVER YOU ARE...
SAVES THE DAY!
FASTEST MAN ALIVE RACE!!!
HEROES!
His name is Colin, please keep him safe and love him always
...HAPPY MOTHER'S DAY.
MAKE A RESERVATION TO JOIN US ON THE NEXT PAGE AS WE CELEBRATE FATHER'S DAY!

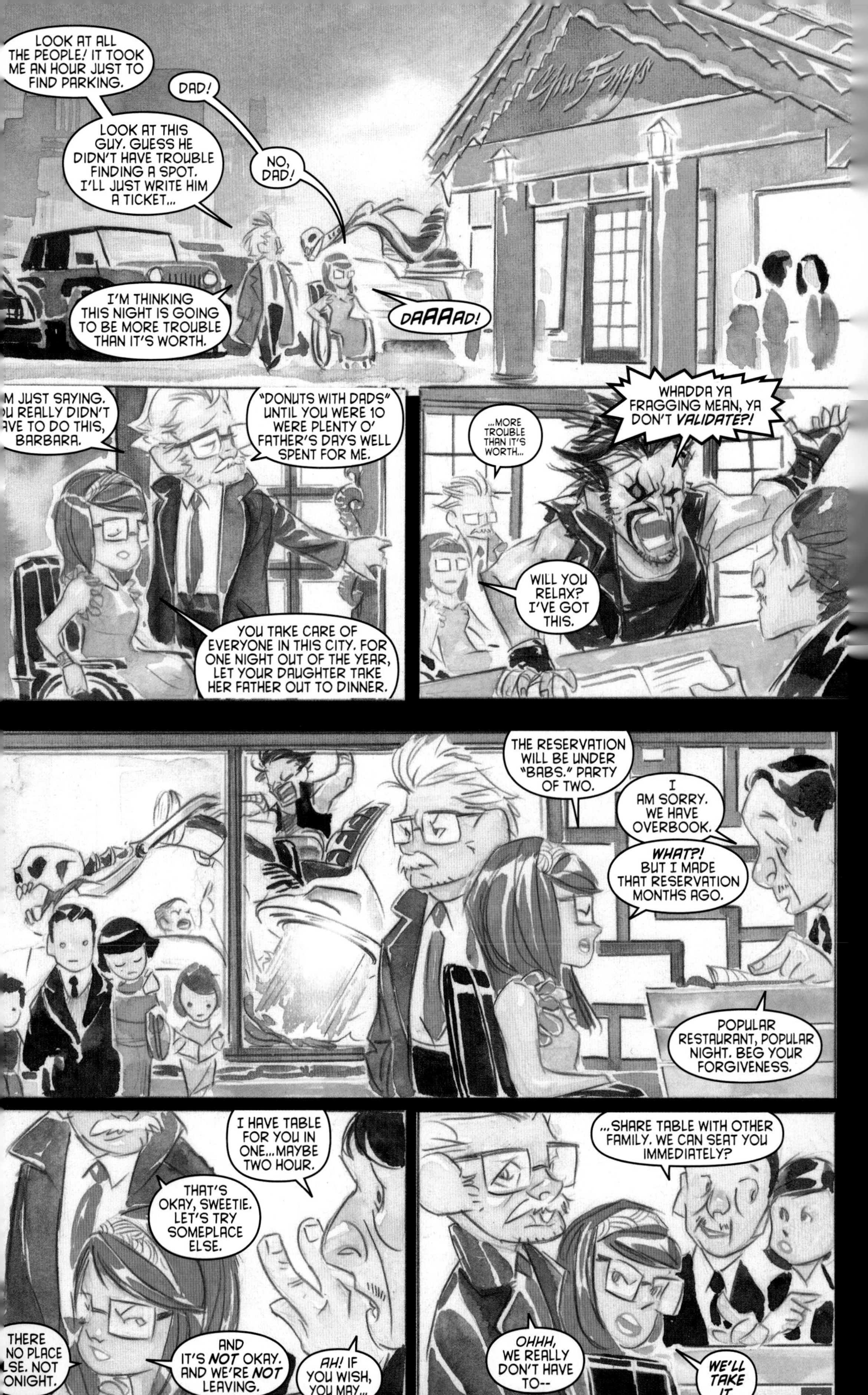
LOOK AT ALL THE PEOPLE! IT TOOK ME AN HOUR JUST TO FIND PARKING.
DAD!
LOOK AT THIS GUY. GUESS HE DIDN'T HAVE TROUBLE FINDING A SPOT. I'LL JUST WRITE HIM A TICKET...
NO, DAD!
I'M THINKING THIS NIGHT IS GOING TO BE MORE TROUBLE THAN IT'S WORTH.
DAAAAD!
M JUST SAYING. U REALLY DIDN'T AVE TO DO THIS, BARBARA.
"DONUTS WITH DADS" UNTIL YOU WERE 10 WERE PLENTY O' FATHER'S DAYS WELL SPENT FOR ME.
YOU TAKE CARE OF EVERYONE IN THIS CITY. FOR ONE NIGHT OUT OF THE YEAR, LET YOUR DAUGHTER TAKE HER FATHER OUT TO DINNER.
...MORE TROUBLE THAN IT'S WORTH...
WHADDA YA FRAGGING MEAN, YA DON'T VALIDATE?!
WILL YOU RELAX? I'VE GOT THIS.
THE RESERVATION WILL BE UNDER "BABS." PARTY OF TWO.
I AM SORRY. WE HAVE OVERBOOK.
WHAT?! BUT I MADE THAT RESERVATION MONTHS AGO.
POPULAR RESTAURANT, POPULAR NIGHT. BEG YOUR FORGIVENESS.
I HAVE TABLE FOR YOU IN ONE...MAYBE TWO HOUR.
THAT'S OKAY, SWEETIE. LET'S TRY SOMEPLACE ELSE.
THERE NO PLACE LSE. NOT ONIGHT.
AND IT'S NOT OKAY. AND WE'RE NOT LEAVING.
AH! IF YOU WISH, YOU MAY...
...SHARE TABLE WITH OTHER FAMILY. WE CAN SEAT YOU IMMEDIATELY?
OHHH, WE REALLY DON'T HAVE TO--
WE'LL TAKE IT.

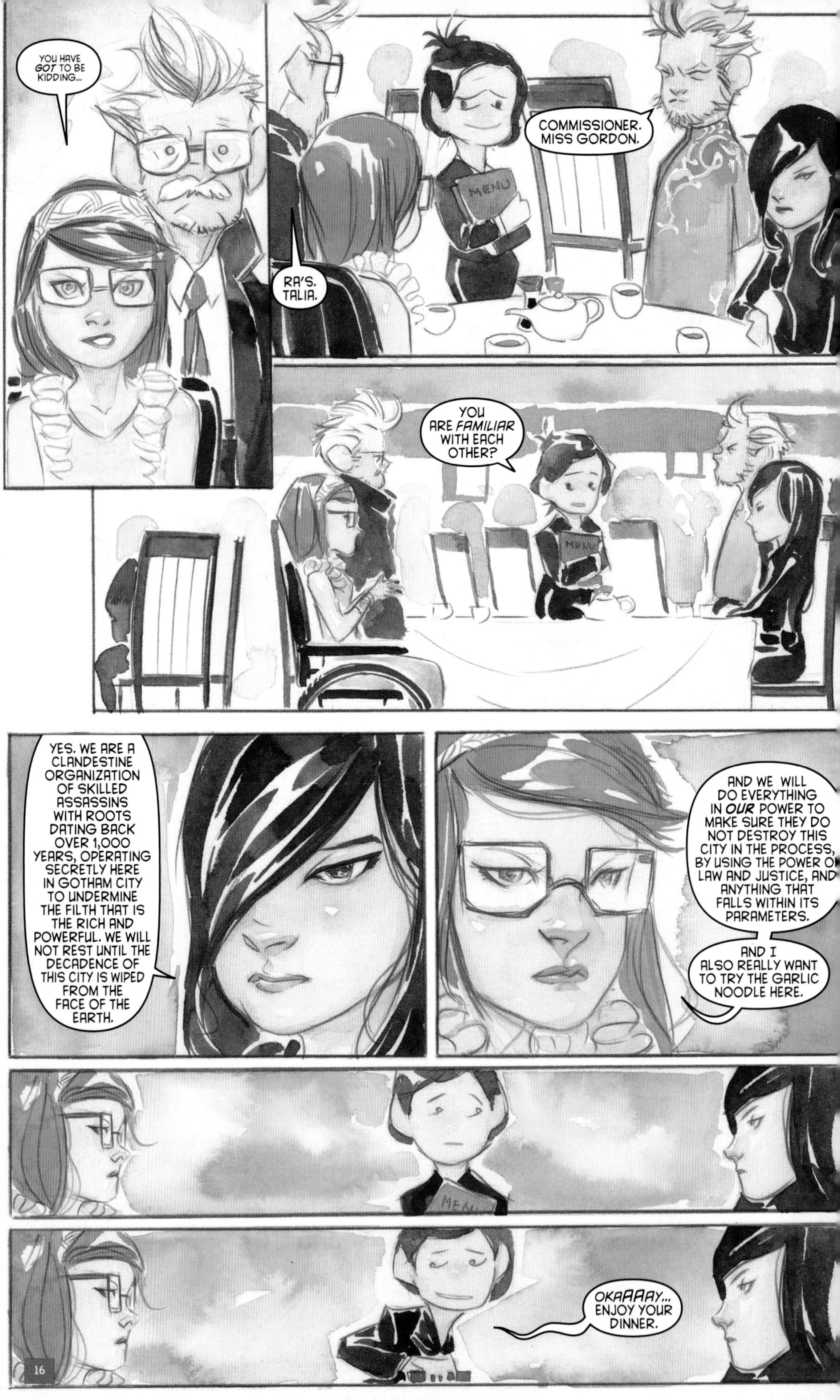
YOU HAVE GOT TO BE KIDDING...
COMMISSIONER. MISS GORDON.
RA'S. TALIA.
YOU ARE FAMILIAR WITH EACH OTHER?
YES. WE ARE A CLANDESTINE ORGANIZATION OF SKILLED ASSASSINS WITH ROOTS DATING BACK OVER 1,000 YEARS, OPERATING SECRETLY HERE IN GOTHAM CITY TO UNDERMINE THE FILTH THAT IS THE RICH AND POWERFUL. WE WILL NOT REST UNTIL THE DECADENCE OF THIS CITY IS WIPED FROM THE FACE OF THE EARTH.
AND WE WILL DO EVERYTHING IN OUR POWER TO MAKE SURE THEY DO NOT DESTROY THIS CITY IN THE PROCESS, BY USING THE POWER OF LAW AND JUSTICE, AND ANYTHING THAT FALLS WITHIN ITS PARAMETERS.
AND I ALSO REALLY WANT TO TRY THE GARLIC NOODLE HERE.
OKAAAAY... ENJOY YOUR DINNER.

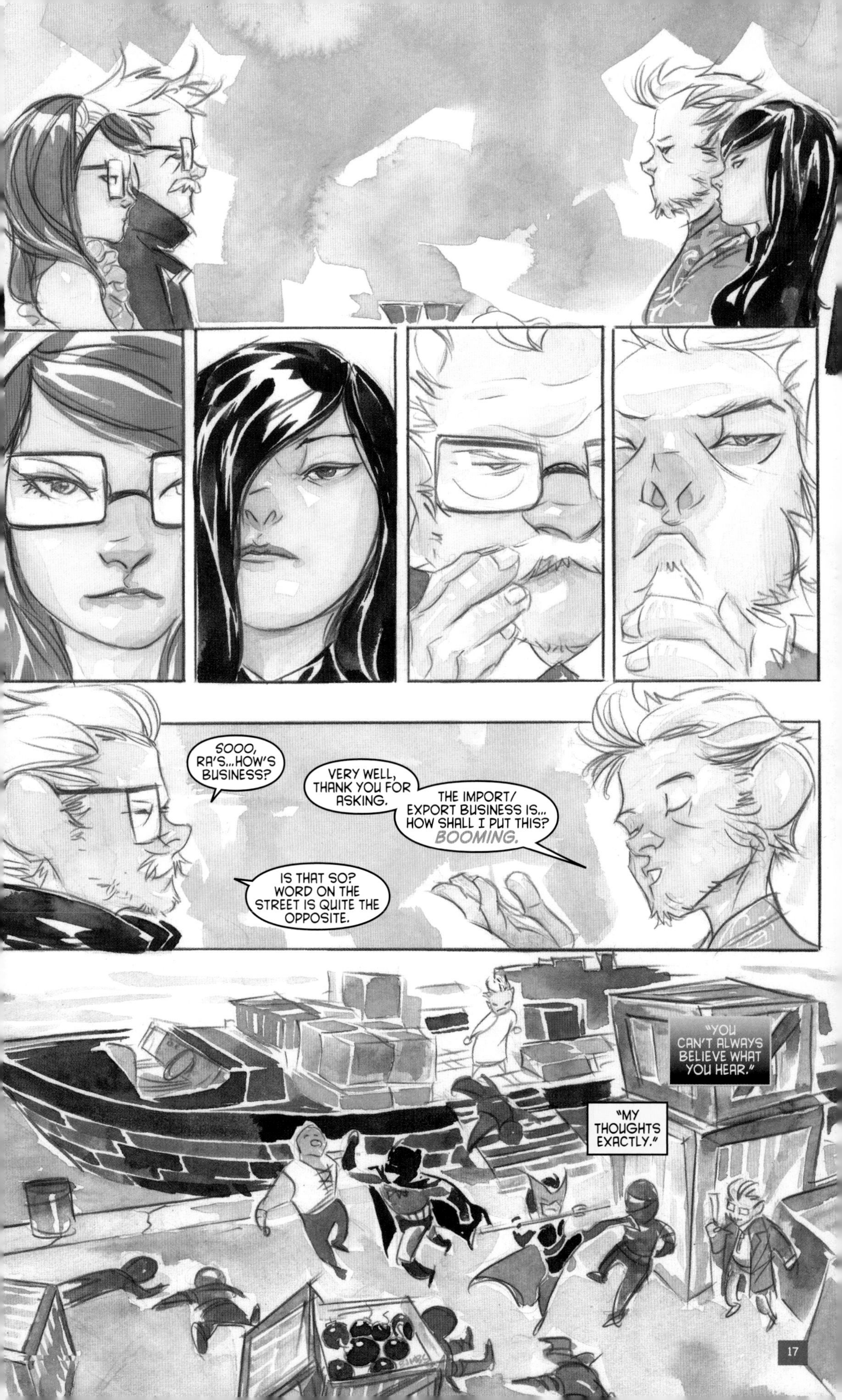
SOOO, RA'S...HOW'S BUSINESS?
VERY WELL, THANK YOU FOR ASKING.
THE IMPORT/ EXPORT BUSINESS IS... HOW SHALL I PUT THIS? *BOOMING.*
IS THAT SO? WORD ON THE STREET IS QUITE THE OPPOSITE.
"YOU CAN'T ALWAYS BELIEVE WHAT YOU HEAR."
"MY THOUGHTS EXACTLY."

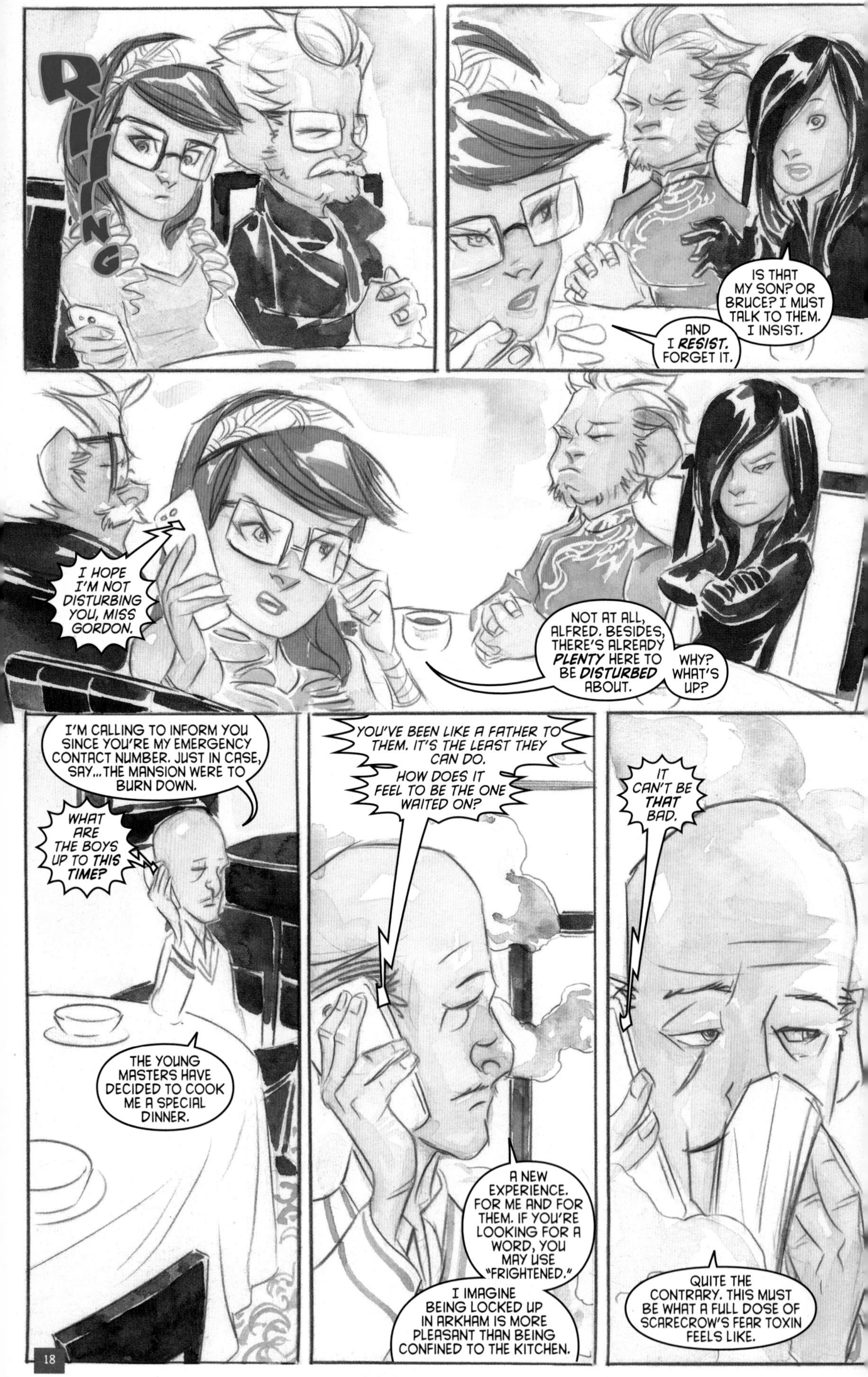
RIIING
IS THAT MY SON? OR BRUCE? I MUST TALK TO THEM. I INSIST.
AND I RESIST. FORGET IT.
I HOPE I'M NOT DISTURBING YOU, MISS GORDON.
NOT AT ALL, ALFRED. BESIDES, THERE'S ALREADY PLENTY HERE TO BE DISTURBED ABOUT.
WHY? WHAT'S UP?
I'M CALLING TO INFORM YOU SINCE YOU'RE MY EMERGENCY CONTACT NUMBER. JUST IN CASE, SAY... THE MANSION WERE TO BURN DOWN.
WHAT ARE THE BOYS UP TO THIS TIME?
THE YOUNG MASTERS HAVE DECIDED TO COOK ME A SPECIAL DINNER.
YOU'VE BEEN LIKE A FATHER TO THEM. IT'S THE LEAST THEY CAN DO.
HOW DOES IT FEEL TO BE THE ONE WAITED ON?
A NEW EXPERIENCE. FOR ME AND FOR THEM. IF YOU'RE LOOKING FOR A WORD, YOU MAY USE "FRIGHTENED."
I IMAGINE BEING LOCKED UP IN ARKHAM IS MORE PLEASANT THAN BEING CONFINED TO THE KITCHEN.
IT CAN'T BE THAT BAD.
QUITE THE CONTRARY. THIS MUST BE WHAT A FULL DOSE OF SCARECROW'S FEAR TOXIN FEELS LIKE.

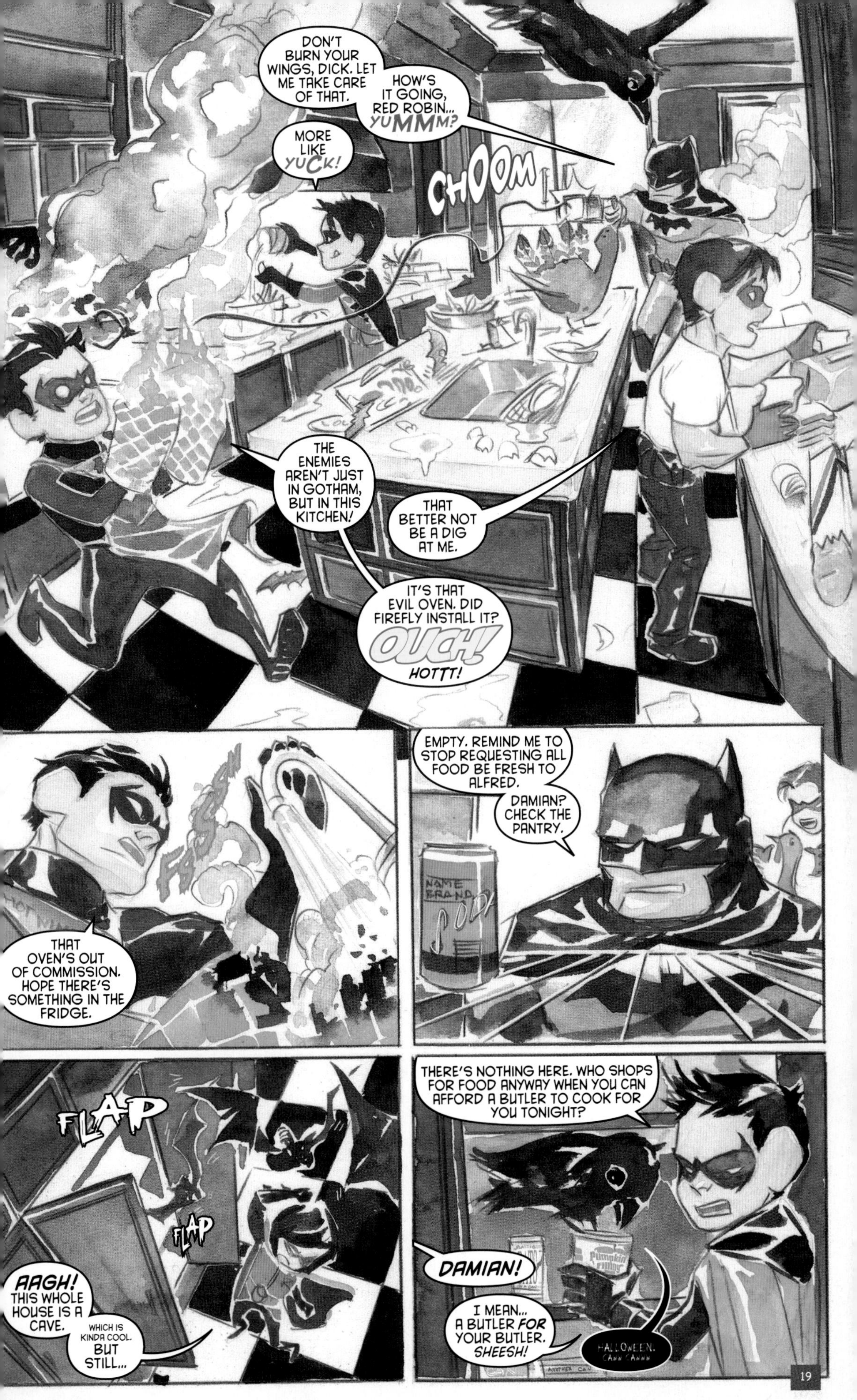
DON'T BURN YOUR WINGS, DICK. LET ME TAKE CARE OF THAT.
HOW'S IT GOING, RED ROBIN... YUMMMM?
MORE LIKE YUCK!
CHOOM
THE ENEMIES AREN'T JUST IN GOTHAM, BUT IN THIS KITCHEN!
THAT BETTER NOT BE A DIG AT ME.
IT'S THAT EVIL OVEN. DID FIREFLY INSTALL IT?
OUCH!
HOTTT!
THAT OVEN'S OUT OF COMMISSION. HOPE THERE'S SOMETHING IN THE FRIDGE.
EMPTY. REMIND ME TO STOP REQUESTING ALL FOOD BE FRESH TO ALFRED.
DAMIAN? CHECK THE PANTRY.
NAME BRAND SODA
FLAP
FLAP
AAGH! THIS WHOLE HOUSE IS A CAVE.
WHICH IS KINDA COOL. BUT STILL...
THERE'S NOTHING HERE. WHO SHOPS FOR FOOD ANYWAY WHEN YOU CAN AFFORD A BUTLER TO COOK FOR YOU TONIGHT?
DAMIAN!
I MEAN... A BUTLER FOR YOUR BUTLER. SHEESH!
HALLOWEEN.

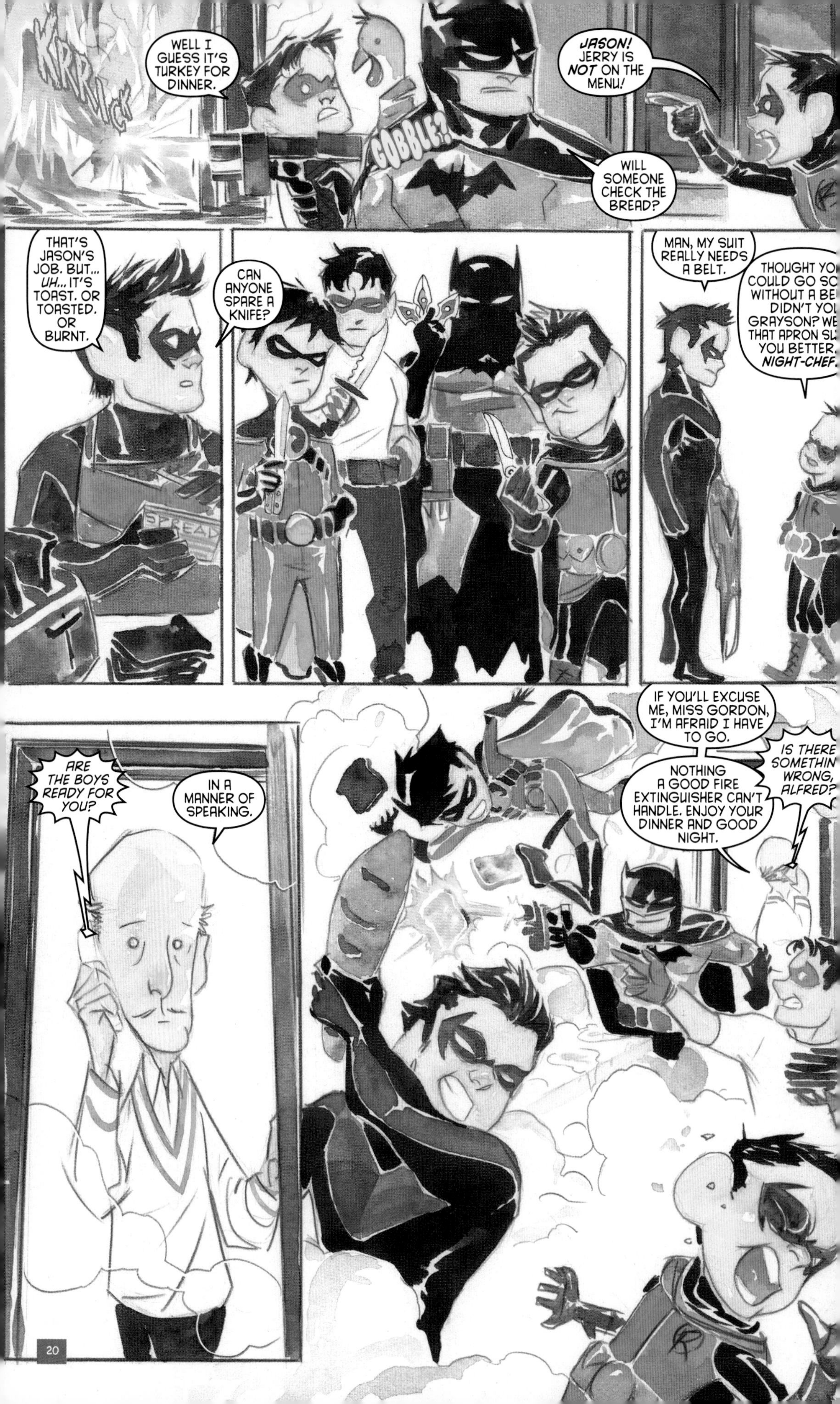
KRRRUNCH
WELL I GUESS IT'S TURKEY FOR DINNER.
GOBBLE?
JASON! JERRY IS NOT ON THE MENU!
WILL SOMEONE CHECK THE BREAD?
THAT'S JASON'S JOB. BUT... UH... IT'S TOAST. OR TOASTED. OR BURNT.
SPREAD
CAN ANYONE SPARE A KNIFE?
MAN, MY SUIT REALLY NEEDS A BELT.
ARE THE BOYS READY FOR YOU?
IN A MANNER OF SPEAKING.
IF YOU'LL EXCUSE ME, MISS GORDON, I'M AFRAID I HAVE TO GO.
NOTHING A GOOD FIRE EXTINGUISHER CAN'T HANDLE. ENJOY YOUR DINNER AND GOOD NIGHT.

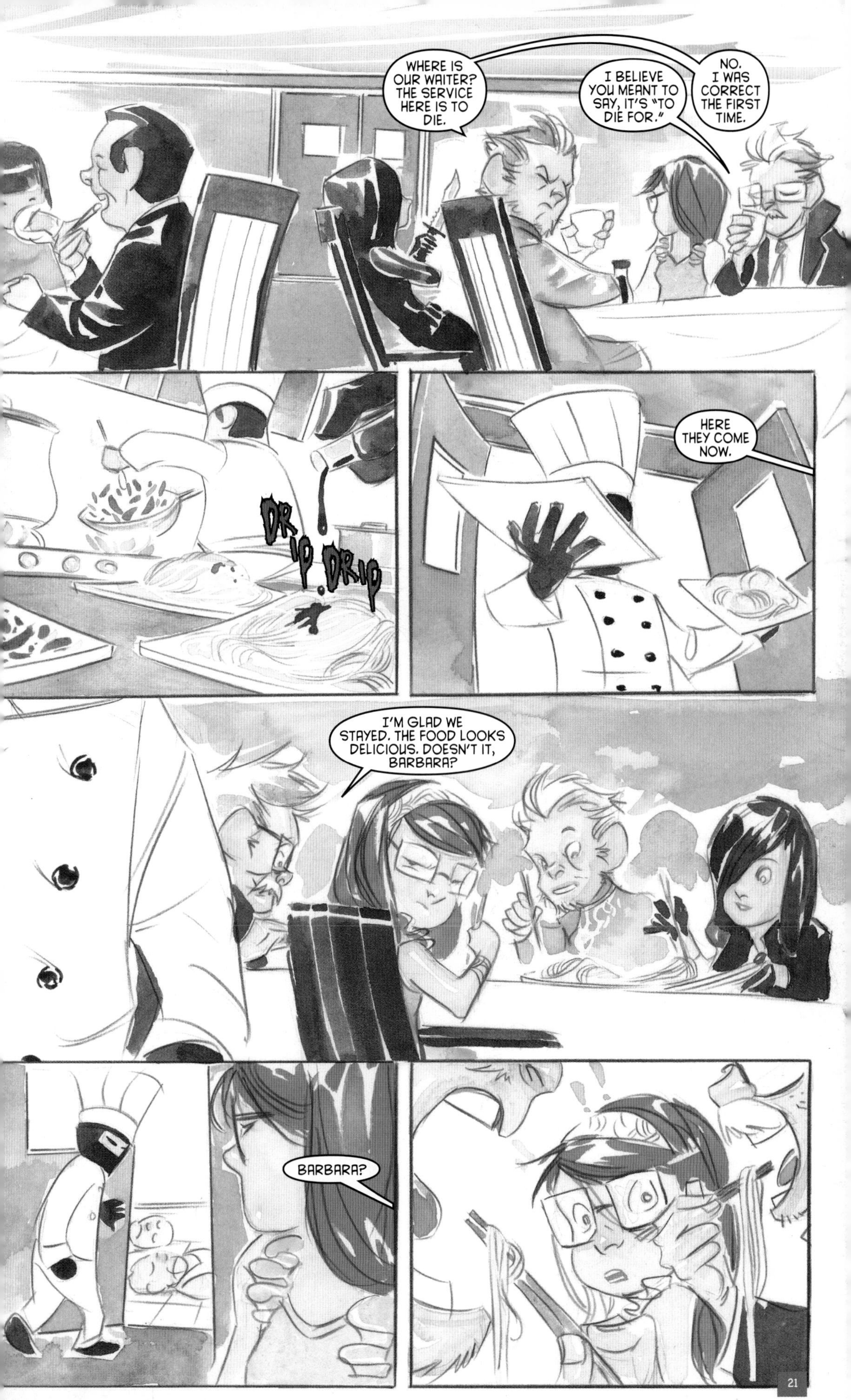
WHERE IS OUR WAITER? THE SERVICE HERE IS TO DIE.
I BELIEVE YOU MEANT TO SAY, IT'S "TO DIE FOR."
NO. I WAS CORRECT THE FIRST TIME.
DRIP DRIP
HERE THEY COME NOW.
I'M GLAD WE STAYED. THE FOOD LOOKS DELICIOUS. DOESN'T IT, BARBARA?
BARBARA?

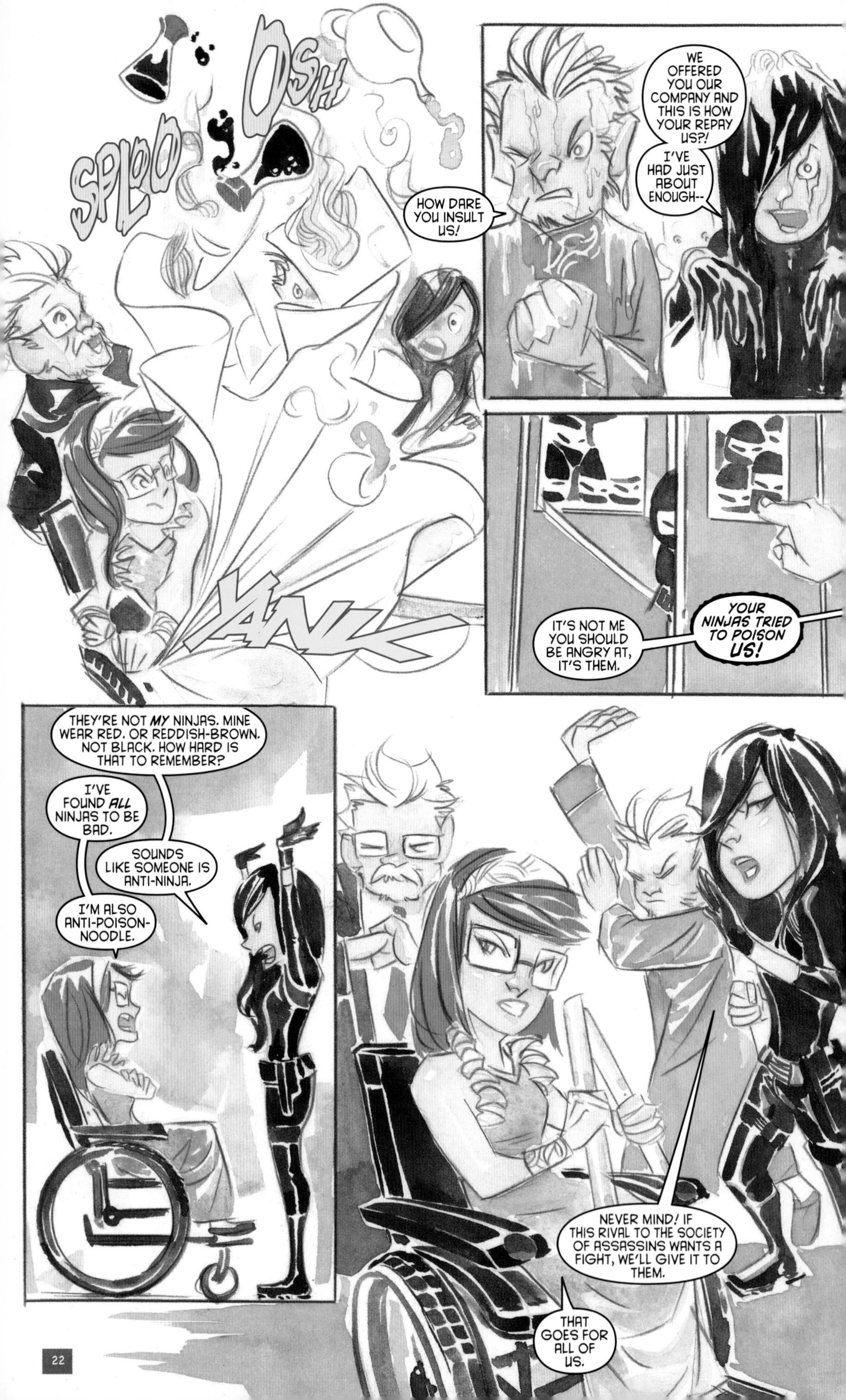
SPLOOSH
HOW DARE YOU INSULT US!
WE OFFERED YOU OUR COMPANY AND THIS IS HOW YOUR REPAY US?!
I'VE HAD JUST ABOUT ENOUGH--
YANK
IT'S NOT ME YOU SHOULD BE ANGRY AT, IT'S THEM.
YOUR NINJAS TRIED TO POISON US!
THEY'RE NOT MY NINJAS. MINE WEAR RED. OR REDDISH-BROWN. NOT BLACK. HOW HARD IS THAT TO REMEMBER?
I'VE FOUND ALL NINJAS TO BE BAD.
SOUNDS LIKE SOMEONE IS ANTI-NINJA.
I'M ALSO ANTI-POISON-NOODLE.
NEVER MIND! IF THIS RIVAL TO THE SOCIETY OF ASSASSINS WANTS A FIGHT, WE'LL GIVE IT TO THEM.
THAT GOES FOR ALL OF US.

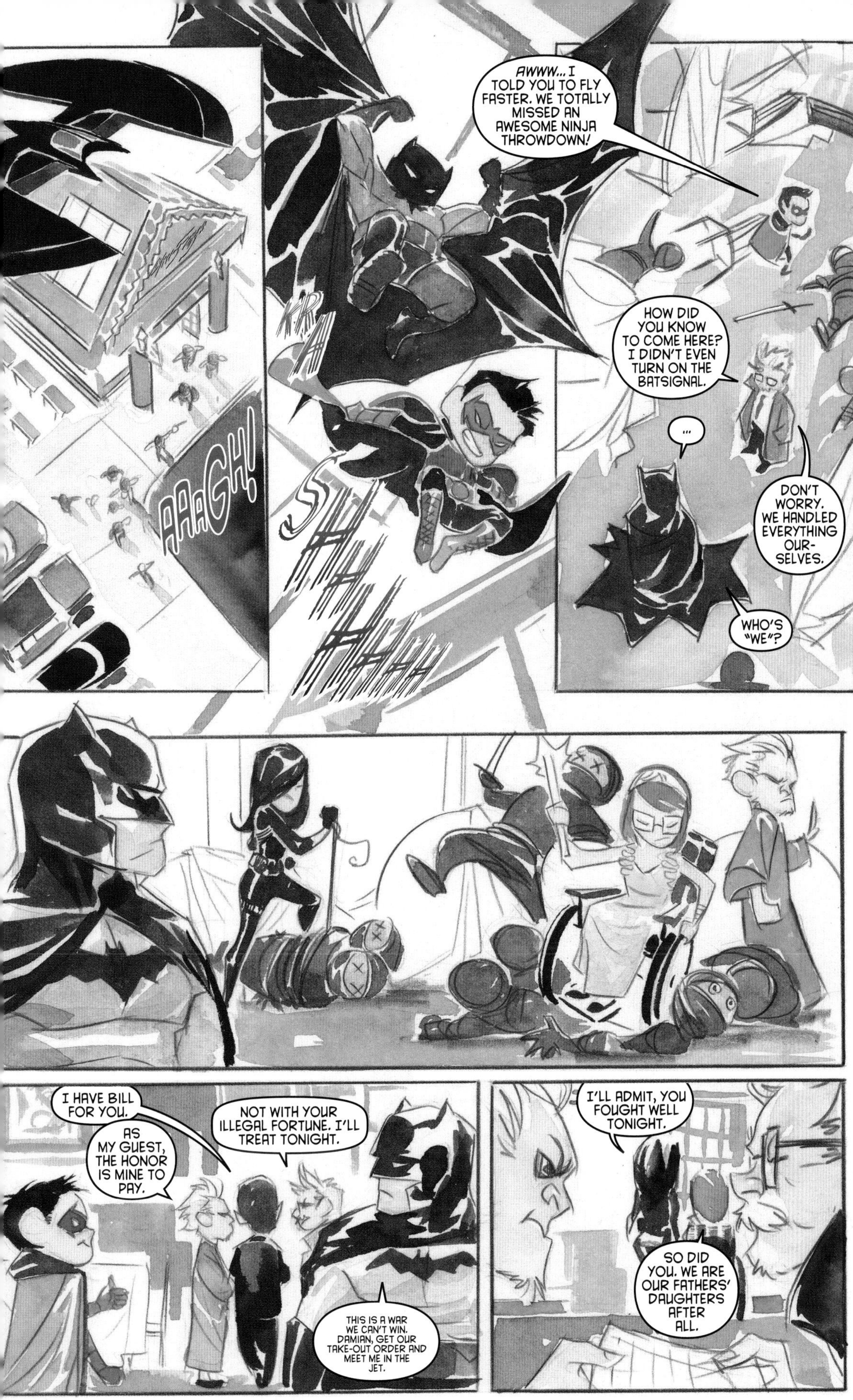
AAAGH!
AWWW... I TOLD YOU TO FLY FASTER. WE TOTALLY MISSED AN AWESOME NINJA THROWDOWN!
KRA
SSHHHHHHHHAAAAAH
HOW DID YOU KNOW TO COME HERE? I DIDN'T EVEN TURN ON THE BATSIGNAL.
...
DON'T WORRY. WE HANDLED EVERYTHING OUR-SELVES.
WHO'S "WE"?
I HAVE BILL FOR YOU.
AS MY GUEST, THE HONOR IS MINE TO PAY.
NOT WITH YOUR ILLEGAL FORTUNE. I'LL TREAT TONIGHT.
THIS IS A WAR WE CAN'T WIN. DAMIAN, GET OUR TAKE-OUT ORDER AND MEET ME IN THE JET.
I'LL ADMIT, YOU FOUGHT WELL TONIGHT.
SO DID YOU. WE ARE OUR FATHERS' DAUGHTERS AFTER ALL.

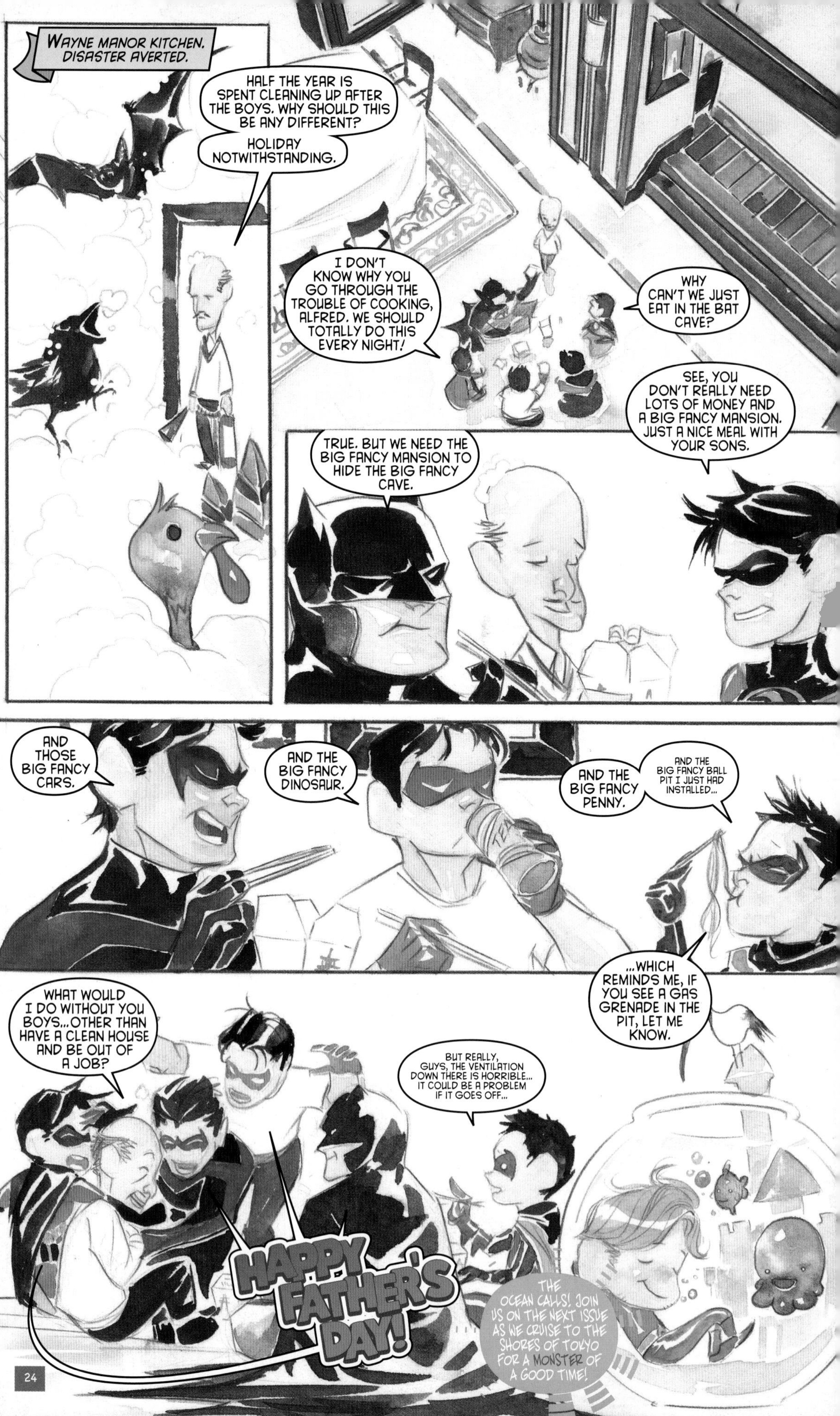
WAYNE MANOR KITCHEN. DISASTER AVERTED.
HALF THE YEAR IS SPENT CLEANING UP AFTER THE BOYS. WHY SHOULD THIS BE ANY DIFFERENT?
HOLIDAY NOTWITHSTANDING.
I DON'T KNOW WHY YOU GO THROUGH THE TROUBLE OF COOKING, ALFRED. WE SHOULD TOTALLY DO THIS EVERY NIGHT!
WHY CAN'T WE JUST EAT IN THE BAT CAVE?
SEE, YOU DON'T REALLY NEED LOTS OF MONEY AND A BIG FANCY MANSION. JUST A NICE MEAL WITH YOUR SONS.
TRUE. BUT WE NEED THE BIG FANCY MANSION TO HIDE THE BIG FANCY CAVE.
AND THOSE BIG FANCY CARS.
AND THE BIG FANCY DINOSAUR.
AND THE BIG FANCY PENNY.
AND THE BIG FANCY BALL PIT I JUST HAD INSTALLED...
...WHICH REMINDS ME, IF YOU SEE A GAS GRENADE IN THE PIT, LET ME KNOW.
WHAT WOULD I DO WITHOUT YOU BOYS...OTHER THAN HAVE A CLEAN HOUSE AND BE OUT OF A JOB?
BUT REALLY, GUYS, THE VENTILATION DOWN THERE IS HORRIBLE... IT COULD BE A PROBLEM IF IT GOES OFF...
HAPPY FATHER'S DAY!
THE OCEAN CALLS! JOIN US ON THE NEXT ISSUE AS WE CRUISE TO THE SHORES OF TOKYO FOR A MONSTER OF A GOOD TIME!

CREATORS

DUSTIN NGUYEN — CO-WRITER & ILLUSTRATOR

Dustin Nguyen is an American comic artist whose body of work includes Wildcats v3.0, The Authority Revolution, Batman, Superman/Batman, Detective Comics, Batgirl, and his creator owned project Manifest Eternity. Currently, he produces all the art for Batman: Li'l Gotham, which is also written by himself and Derek Fridolfs. Outside of comics, Dustin moonlights as a conceptual artist for toys, games, and animation. In his spare time, he enjoys sleeping, driving, and sketching things he loves.

DEREK FRIDOLFS — CO-WRITER

Derek Fridolfs is a comic book writer, inker, and artist. He resides in Gotham--present and future.

GLOSSARY

allergies (AL-er-jeez)--sneezing, itching, or rashes that occurs due to heightened sensitivities to certain substances, situations, or physical states that typically don't affect most people

averted (uh-VER-tid)--prevented from happening, or avoided

brainwashed (BRAYN-washd)--changed someone's ideas or perspectives by force or manipulation

clandestine (CLAN-duh-stine)--done in secret

confined (kuhn-FIND)--kept within limits or imprisoned

indigestion (in-duh-JEST-shuhn)--a case or attack of a burning or uncomfortable feeling in the upper stomach

orphanage (OR-fuh-nij)--an institution for the care of orphans (children without parents)

mutilate (MYOO-tuh-late)--to cut off or destroy a necessary part

rival (RYE-vuhl)--a rival is someone who is trying to get what only one can have but multiple people want

teleportation (tel-uh-pore-TAY-shuhn)--the fictional ability to instantly travel from one place to another

validate (VAL-uh-date)--to make valid or legitimate

VISUAL QUESTIONS & PROMPTS

1. Batman is the only member of the Justice League who does not have superpowers. What skills, abilities, or resources does he have that makes him a worthwhile member of the team?

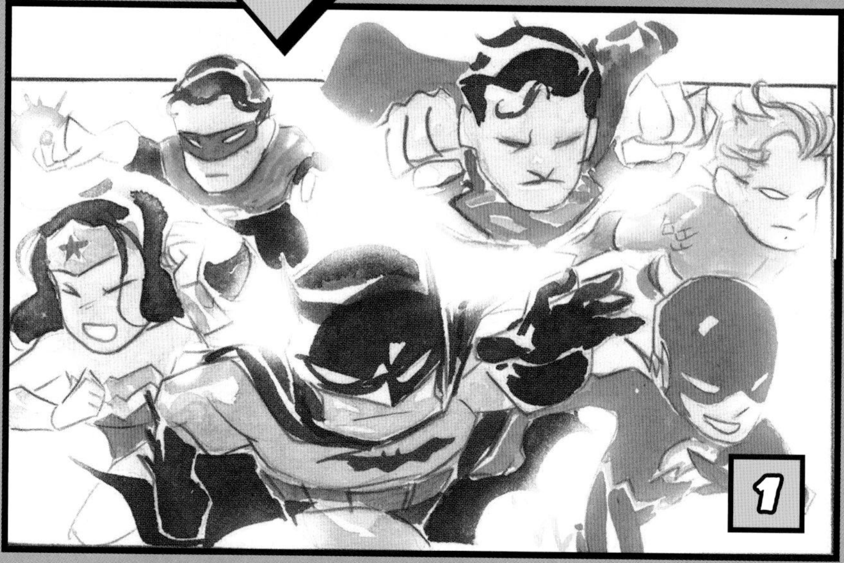
1

2. What happened to Damian on page 11?

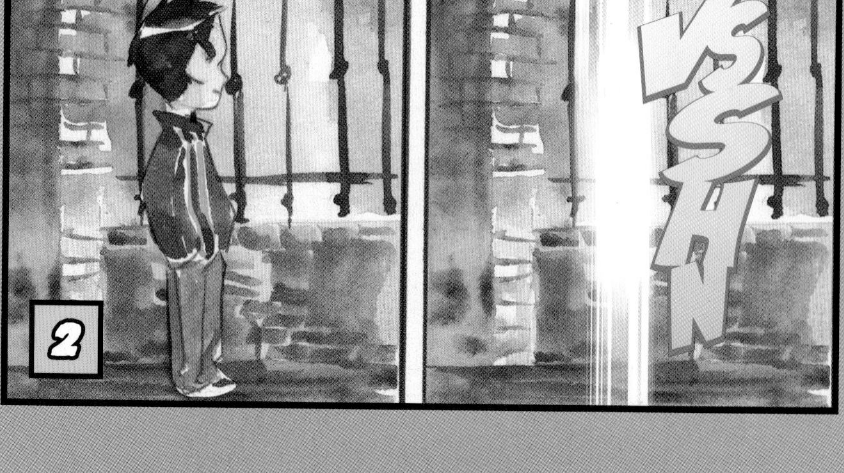
2
VSSHN

3. Based on the facial expressions of Ra's, Talia, Barbara, Gordon, and the waitress, how do you think they all feel after being seated together?

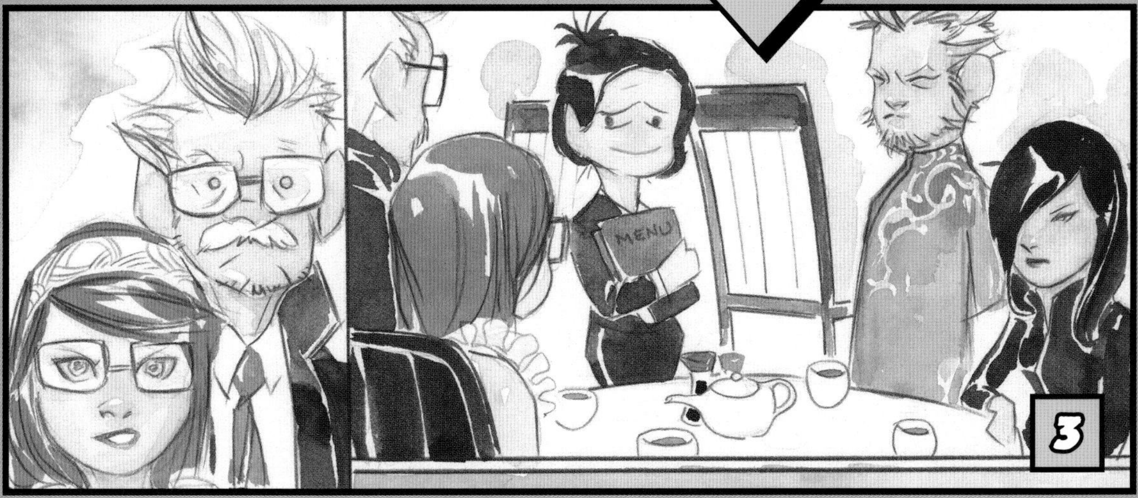
MENU
3

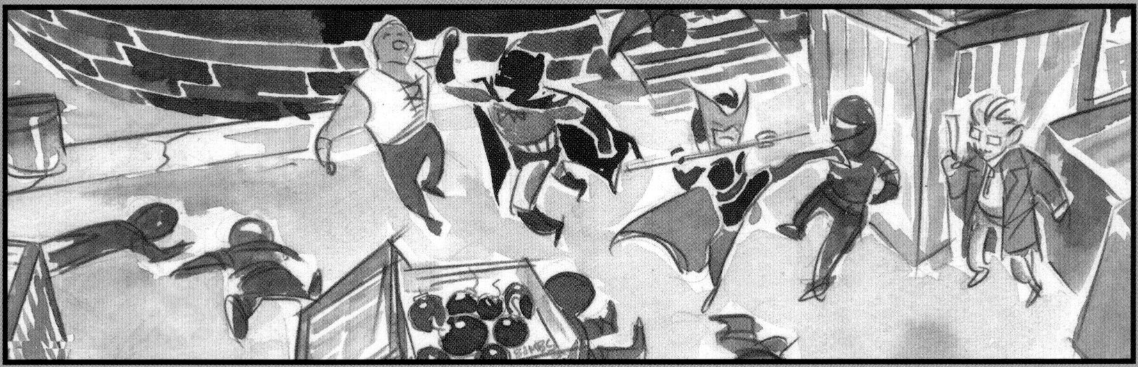

4. Why is there a dotted line around Damian's speech bubble in this panel?

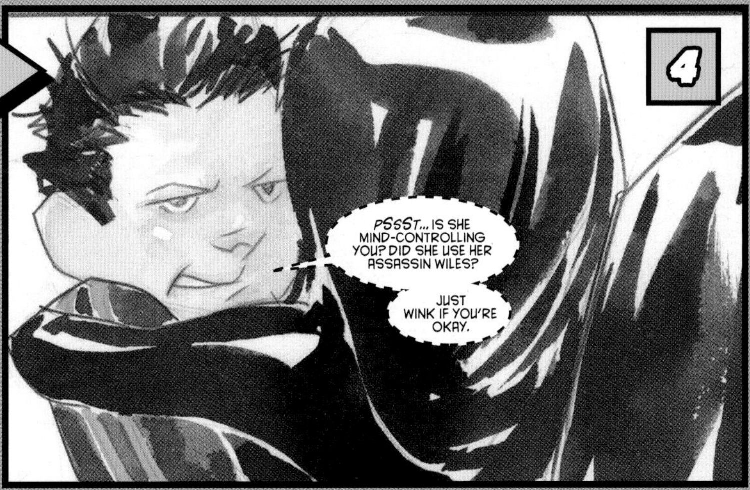
4
PSSST... IS SHE MIND-CONTROLLING YOU? DID SHE USE HER ASSASSIN WILES?
JUST WINK IF YOU'RE OKAY.

BATMAN™ LI'L GOTHAM

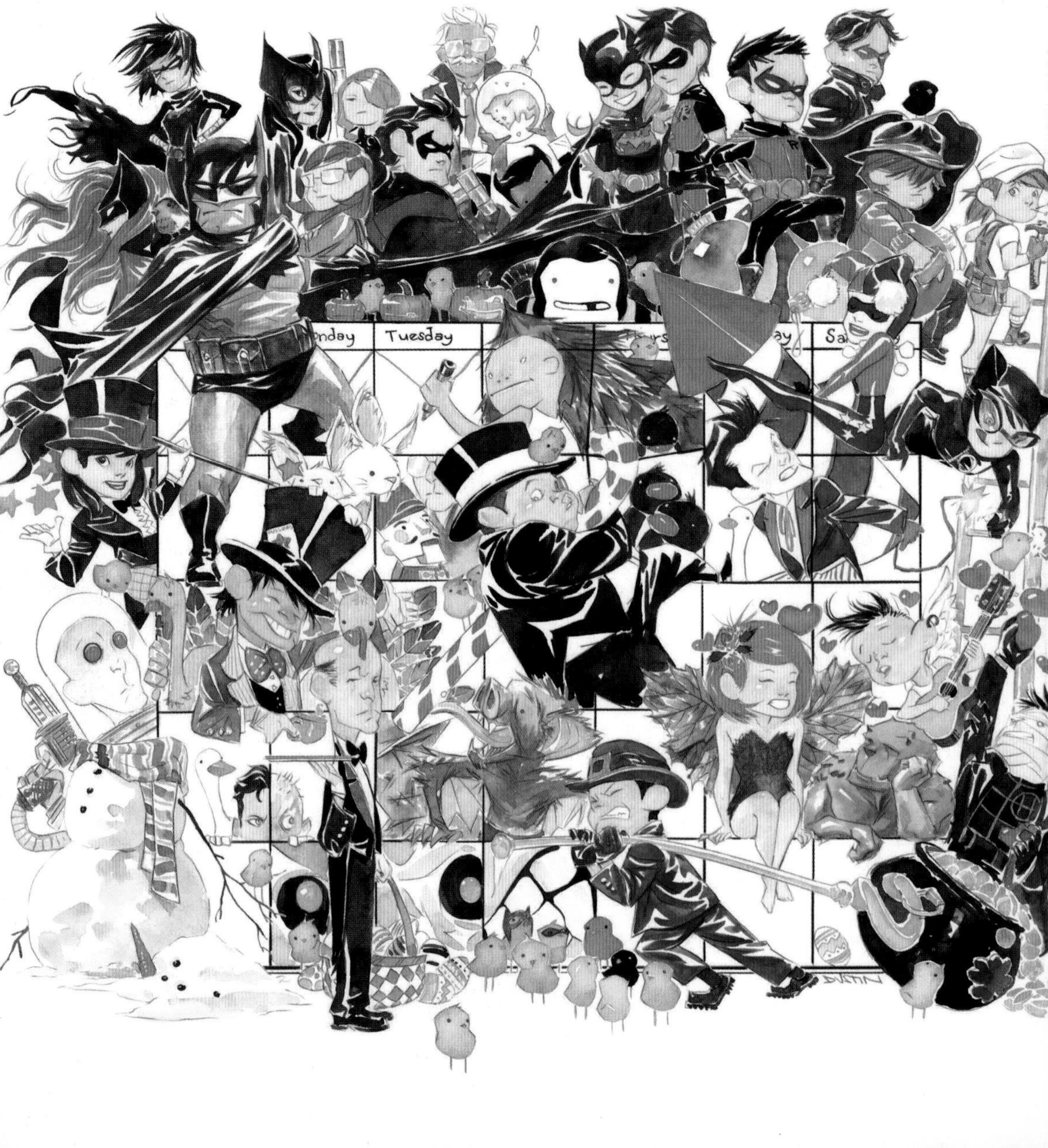
Tuesday
DUSTIN

READ THEM ALL!

DC COMICS
BATMAN
LI'L GOTHAM
NGUYEN
FRIDOLFS
HALLOWEEN AND THANKSGIVING

DC COMICS
BATMAN
LI'L GOTHAM
CHRISTMAS AND NEW YEAR'S EVE
NGUYEN • FRIDOLFS

DC COMICS
BATMAN
LI'L GOTHAM
NGUYEN
FRIDOLFS
VALENTINE'S DAY AND THE LUNAR NEW YEAR

DC COMICS
BATMAN
LI'L GOTHAM
ST. PATRICK'S DAY AND EASTER
NGUYEN • FRIDOLFS

DC COMICS
BATMAN
LI'L GOTHAM
NGUYEN
FRIDOLFS
APRIL SHOWERS AND CINCO DE MAYO

DC COMICS
BATMAN
LI'L GOTHAM
NGUYEN
FRIDOLFS
MOTHER'S DAY AND FATHER'S DAY

only from...

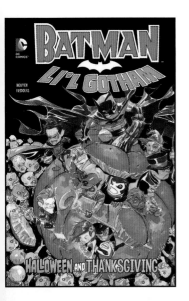

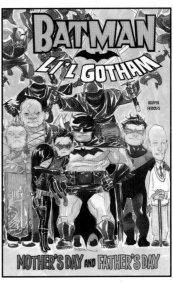

BATMAN™
LI'L GOTHAM

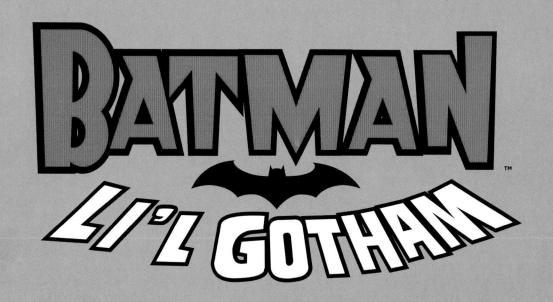